A Match Made in Heaven

You know when you find the one...

A complete billionaire romance, brought to you by Ashlie Brooks of African American Club.

Janelle Peters didn't know what to expect from her first produced game show, but it certainly wasn't to end up starring in it!

Right before the first episode of Match Made In Heaven goes to air, one of the female contestants backs out and Janelle has no choice but to step in.

Handsome bachelor Reece James is instructed to vote her off in the first round, but when they get to talking on the show she finds out they have more in common than she ever thought possible.

Soon Reece and Janelle start to spend a lot of off-camera time together, and they quickly realize that they're falling head over heels in love.

However, there's one thing that Janelle doesn't know about Reece, and he isn't sure how to break the news...

Are the two a match made in heaven?

Or will Reece's secret be too much for Janelle to handle?

Find out in this steamy and secretive billionaire romance by Ashlie Brooks.

Suitable for over 18s only due to sex scenes so hot, you won't ever want anybody to yell 'cut'!

Get Free Romance eBooks!

Hi there. As a special thank you for buying this book, for a limited time I want to send you some great ebooks completely **free of charge** directly to your email! You can get it by going to this page:

www.saucyromancebooks.com/physical

You can see a the cover of these books on the next page:

These ebooks are so exclusive you can't even buy them. When you download them I'll also send you updates when new books like this are available.

Again, that link is:

www.saucyromancebooks.com/physical

ISBN-13: 978-1522924197

ISBN-10: 1522924191

Contents

Chapter 1

"Okay everybody, let's take five and then we'll start recording!"

Janelle's voice rang out in the studio. They'd finished the rehearsal, now it was time for the real thing. Match made in Heaven was Janelle's idea. She'd thought it up a few years ago, but it had been shoved to the bottom of the pile in favor of other reality shows that were more popular with the audience. Now, she had time for her idea.

At twenty-nine, Janelle was more successful than she ever would have guessed. She made a nice amount of money, had her own place, a nice car. Still, it could get difficult working so much. She very rarely had anytime to date and when she did, they didn't seem to ever go well. She knew it wasn't because of her looks; not with her shapely hips, light brown skin, big brown eyes and jet black hair. She was positive it had more to do with the way she acted when she was around someone she didn't know.

"Janelle, we have a problem," Mya said as she walked up with her clipboard in hand, effectively shaking the woman out of her thoughts. "Angela wants to drop out."

"I'm sorry, what?"

"Yeah, she says she doesn't want to do it anymore. Thinks the bachelor is boring or some nonsense like that. She's already packing up her stuff to leave."

Janelle spun on her tall heels before she made her way to the dressing rooms. The other women were sitting by, watching the red haired woman gather her things. Not only was she packing, but by the scowl on her face, Janelle knew that she was angry.

"What's wrong, Angela?"

"What's wrong? Your bachelor is a bore and the contestants are crazy!" She said as she threw a glance at one of the other women in the room. "I don't have time for this. I'm going home."

"Angela please, you signed a contract," Janelle said.

The woman scoffed, picked up her black bag before tossing it over her shoulder. "Sue me."

The woman brushed past Janelle, the loud sound of her footsteps echoing down the hallway. Janelle looked at the other women in the room with a raised eyebrow. Whoever had succeeded in angering Angela wasn't speaking up. She sighed.

"Hang tight, ladies. I have to find a stand in."

Janelle couldn't believe this was happening already. This was the first show that she'd come up with completely on her own, the last thing she wanted was to see it fail. Her first stop was the break room. It smelled like the sugary sweet donuts that adorned it every day as well as the strong smell of brewing coffee.

A few interns were sitting at the table, young, bright eyed women who'd do nicely. Besides, all they had to do was sit in for the taping then Reece could vote her off. It would keep the show on track, that was all she cared about. Janelle cleared her throat, putting on a smile as she walked up to the three women.

"I need a favor," she said, leaning forward with her hands on the table, "I need someone to take Angela's spot on the show. It'll just be this once, then he'll vote you off."

Natalie shook her head. "I'm married," she said pointing to her ring, "my husband would flip."

"Ditto," Tina answered, "except boyfriend and his family already hates me. I'd never hear the end of it."

Janelle turned to the last woman. "Gina?"

"Gay, so very, very gay. I can't even fake an interest."

Janelle hung her head. Just then she heard the tapping of heels. Only one other woman worked there besides the big network execs that sometimes stopped by, Mya. She turned around quickly, a grin on her face.

"Mya..."

"Hell no. I heard you before I even came in here. No, no, no. I work behind the scenes for a reason. I don't want to be on TV."

Janelle slouched into a chair. "I guess that's it. It's all over. My show is ruined."

Mya rolled her eyes. "Will you stop being dramatic? Why don't you just do it?"

"Come again?"

"Take Angela's place! It's your show. Besides, you *are* single."

"Don't remind me," Janelle mumbled burying her face in her hand. When she looked back up, she bit her lip. "It could work though, right? I mean, who'd find out?"

"Exactly," Mya said excitedly. "The show must go on!"

Janelle laughed, shaking her head. "Fine. I can't wear this," she said gesturing to herself.

"Let's get you into wardrobe, then we can do something about that hair and makeup."

"I don't wear makeup," Janelle protested.

"You do today."

Janelle could hear the interns laughing in the break room as she left. "Remind me to not hire them," she said with a shake of her head.

Mya laughed. "You love those interns."

"True."

They walked into wardrobe together. The other contestants were already dressed to kill in dresses that clung tight to their bodies, heels that were tall and had enough cleavage out to distract any man. Janelle started sorting through the clothes with her assistant.

Mya leaned over to her. "Don't they know he can't see them?"

Janelle elbowed her as she stifled a laugh. She picked out a dress as well, but it was different. It was a short sun dress in a dark red color that complemented her golden brown skin. When she slipped it on, it lay against her hips, accentuating every curve of her body. She twisted back and forth in the mirror, tilted her head.

"I don't look half bad," she mumbled.

"Stop checking yourself out. We have to get to hair and makeup."

Despite Mya's words, when Janelle stepped out of the dressing room, the woman stared. Her eyes ran over Janelle's figure slowly. Janelle grinned.

"I know right? I might dress like this more often."

Janelle's usual attire consisted of black, black and more black. Black skirts, black slacks, dark jeans. Occasionally a white blouse found its way into her repertoire but that was few and far between. She followed behind Mya to get her hair fixed next. Generally kept in a bun, the girl immediately took it down.

"Why did you have to take it down?"

"Buns aren't exactly what this audience will want to see," she said as she began to brush through her hair. "Don't worry, I'll make you look good," the girl said with a grin.

Janelle sat in the chair, checking her phone for the time every five minutes. Only when she was lost in her inbox of emails did she forget about the time restraints that she had. Brushes slid over her face as she was told to close one eye then the other. Before she knew it, the girl was telling her to look in the mirror. She did.

The woman in the mirror had thick, wavy black hair that fell just to her breasts. Her eyes were outlined with liner making them look more dramatic along with the mascara. Her skin looked completely smooth, although she knew there was still a scar near her nose from an old accident. Her lips were a matte red, the color bringing out the natural plumpness of them. Janelle sat there staring at herself for so long that the girl had to clear her throat.

"What do you think?"

"Wow," Janelle said as she touched her face. "I look...different."

"I think you look cute," Mya said. "Now, let's get going. Reece is ready."

Janelle nodded as she pushed herself out of the chair. She'd only met Reece twice. Once when he approached her for the position, the second time when she was picking out candidates. She'd settled on Reece because he had such a sweet back story. He was the owner of a small art gallery and painted himself. His family was small, his bank account modest, but he was very sweet. The way he smiled had a way of lighting up the room.

She walked onto the set. The other contestants were already settling on stage, outfitted with their portable mics. As she slipped into a chair, one of the tech guys put one on her as well. All at once the nervousness overtook her. It may not have been real for her, but she'd still be on TV. If they were lucky, it would air in front of millions of people. *Is this what I want to be known as? The first woman to be rejected off of Match Made in Heaven?*

There was no time to rethink her plan as the host of the show walked onto the stage. He wore a dark blue, tailored suit. His hair was impeccable, soft blond strands of gold and his eyes were pools of blue. He grinned at Janelle. She rolled her eyes.

Clark was her oldest friend. He'd stood by her side since they were in diapers and knew everything about her. They'd gone to the same schools, the same colleges until they both ended up in damn near the same careers. However, while Janelle liked to stay behind the scenes, Clark was constantly in the limelight. He preferred it that way.

"Welcome to *Match Made in Heaven*, a modern day matchmaking show. During the course of this show you'll get to know our bachelor, but you won't get to see him. He's behind that curtain," the man pointed, the women smiling or giggling as they glanced at the red curtain, "and he's ready to meet our guests. Now, the only thing they're allowed to know is his name, Reece. However, they know nothing else about him. They'll get to ask him questions and at the end of the round he can ask each guest one question in return. Are you ready Reece?"

"Ready," a deep voice called from the other side of the curtain.

"Ladies?"

"Ready!" The women's voices said in unison.

"Good, let's get started! Now, our first guest is Zoey," Clark started.

Janelle was already drifting. As the women around her asked Reece questions, she was thinking about production. They would have to edit the tapes, tomorrow would be round two. She vaguely wondered if she would have enough time to make dinner or if she'd have to pickup takeout when she heard her name being called.

"Tara, do you have a question for Reece?"

The woman snapped back to reality. Tara, they didn't have a Tara. It slowly sunk in that Clark was talking about her. She swallowed thickly, it suddenly felt as though she had a throat of saw dust. She cleared her throat and asked the first question that popped into her mind.

"What's your go to meal when you're home?"

Reece was quiet for a moment before he chuckled. "I like to think I'm pretty good in the kitchen. When I'm home, I like to try cuisines from different cultures. I don't really have a go to meal, but usually some kind of pasta is on the menu. I'm very active so I eat for my nightly runs."

Janelle nodded, a smile on her face. "That's actually pretty cool."

Clark moved on to the next guest, but she was thinking about Reece. She liked to go on runs too, every morning before work and after dinner too if she had time. *We have something in common.*

The next round started and Reece began to ask each of them a question. Janelle was distracted once again. She wanted to check her watch badly to see what time it was. They couldn't go over the allotted time or there would be a bunch of editing that needed to be done.

"Tara," Reece said, "what do you consider the most influential time period in history?"

"The Renaissance period, mostly 1483 to 1513. It was the age where we had some great art introduced to the world. Leonardo, Michelangelo, Botticelli. Not to mention it was the discovery of the New World."

"Wow."

Janelle winced. "That was probably incredibly nerdy."

Reece laughed, that same deep timbered chuckle. "Not at all. I'm something of a history enthusiast myself. Thank you."

Clark was once again smiling at the women as he wrapped up the show. As soon as they got them all clear, Janelle hopped from her seat and headed to the dressing room. The other women followed behind her. She was glad that it had gone so smoothly, but her mind couldn't stop going back to Reece. What were the odds that she'd found a fellow runner and history buff to be on the show? It certainly made him more intriguing in her eyes.

Janelle slipped back into her clothes, before typing her hair up in a messy bun. Grabbing her clipboard, she went over a few details with Mya before she headed off in search of Reece. She knocked on the door, waiting until he opened it. She smiled.

"How was it?" She asked stepping into the room.

"I enjoyed myself. The ladies really seem interesting. I'm glad I did this," he said closing the door before he walked back over. "That Tara was really something."

Janelle laughed awkwardly as she sat down. The man in front of her was impressive to say the least. He was six-two with chocolate brown skin and brown eyes. His shoulders were wide, the purple button down shirt that he wore hinting at an abundance of muscles underneath. Facial hair covered his chin and his black hair was kept short. She had to admit, he was an attractive man.

"Actually, I wanted to talk to you about that."

Reece took a spot in his chair. "What's going on?"

Janelle sighed. "There isn't a Tara. One of our guests dropped out and we had to find a replacement quickly. Well, no one else could fill in, so I had to do it."

The man's eyes went wide as he pointed to her. "You mean, that was you?"

She nodded. "Of course, you can vote me out first so that you can focus on the other contestants. I just wanted to let you know."

The man nodded slowly. He was clearly thinking about something, but it was hard to tell what that was. He rubbed a hand over his chin.

"We'll have a few re-shoots tomorrow probably," Janelle said trying to break the silence in the room. "Then on the next episode you can let me go. I know it's a bit of a pain to have your options cut down by one, but it was the best we could do on such short notice."

He nodded again. "That's fine, of course," he stood up. "So, were your answers made up or..."

Janelle smiled. "No, those were mine. I said the first thing that came to my mind for that history stuff. Although it is nice to meet someone else who's as interested in history as I am."

"I keep a copy of History of the World on my bedside table."

"I do too!" Janelle said a little more loudly than she'd meant to. She laughed. "I mean, I have for a long time. I've read it so many times that it's pretty much falling apart at this point."

"I know exactly what you mean. I just had to replace my copy not too long ago," he chuckled. "I hope this isn't too forward, but do you think we could grab a cup of coffee? Talk history?"

"I think that would be great," she said as she stood up. "How about tomorrow night?"

"I was thinking more along the lines of right now."

Janelle grinned. "I have to review the tapes, but I could be out of here at say," she glanced at her watch, "seven?"

"Deal. Meet me at Hifi?"

"Sounds good," she said as she walked out of his dressing room, closing the door behind her.

On the other side of the door, Janelle shook her head and smiled. She hadn't gone out in a while, besides the occasional dinner dates with Clark. The woman bit her lip. It would have been better if it were a date. *Yeah right, he came on the show for a reason.* Besides, she reasoned, there were four other women just waiting for him to choose them.

She walked into production where Mya was already in front of the screen going over the tape. The woman's headset lay on the desk as she gazed at the feed. Janelle watched another monitor, one showing the contestants leaving for the day. They weren't allowed to see each other before the finale and she didn't want anyone trying to change that. Once they were clear, she settled into a chair.

"Can you run and tell Reece that he can leave now?"

"Sure," Mya said, rising out of her chair slowly before she paused the feed. "I'll be right back."

Janelle thought back to Reece. He'd almost seemed disappointed when she'd told him to vote her off of the show. This time, she laughed at herself as she rolled through the footage. *Stop being ridiculous.* Still, it would have been nice for a guy like that to take a real interest in her she thought.

When Mya came back, they began to look through the footage together. She gazed up partway through their work to see

Reece leaving the building. He walked out to a sleek, black car before pulling out of the parking lot. It gave her a little rush of excitement knowing that she would be meeting up with him soon.

Once the video was edited and the schedule for the next day emailed to the contestants, Janelle headed home. She and Mya walked to their cars together, before she slipped behind the wheel of her car. She started the car, loving the roar of the engine as it turned over. The '64 candy apple red Mustang was her newest present to herself. She loved it. Once Mya pulled out, she followed after her until they parted ways.

Janelle made sure to move relatively close to the studio. Of course in Los Angeles that meant higher rent, but she thought it was worth it. It was a loft style apartment with down to earth furnishings and small on space, but it was home. She pulled into the garage before taking the elevator up to her floor.

As she stepped inside, she glanced at her watch. She had just enough time to shower, change into something comfy and meet Reece for coffee. As she walked through her place, her cat jumped off of her desk. The orange tabby round itself around her ankles almost making her trip as she made her way to the bathroom. Janelle picked him up.

"It was a very good day, Mulder," she said cradling the cat, "The bachelor is really nice. Hot too," she mumbled as she sat the cat back down.

Janelle shed her clothes before she turned on the shower. Stepping in, she sighed as the water hit her skin. It had been a long day, but tomorrow would be too. She didn't take long, forgoing her usually long shower for a short one so she wouldn't be late. When she stepped out, she wrapped a thick, blue towel around her body before padding to her bedroom.

Opening her closet, she looked around for something to wear. She traded in the work wear for a pair of comfortable blue jeans that hugged her hips nicely. A light blue top was pulled over her head before she looked at herself in the mirror. Reaching up, she pulled her hair down out of its bun. It had been a long time since she'd worn anything but the bun or ponytail. Quickly she brushed her hair out, the waves still in place from earlier. Janelle swiped on a little makeup.

"Not bad," she mumbled.

Crouching down, she pet Mulder on the way out the door. She

was both nervous and excited about seeing Reece. The woman had a way of stumbling over her words when she had to talk to new people out of her usual studio setting. The thought that she'd make a fool out of herself in front of him wasn't comforting.

Janelle pulled into Hifi's parking lot a little before seven. She tried to talk herself down. It wasn't a date, it wasn't important, it was just two people meeting for coffee to talk about history. Still, she couldn't help the slight fluttering that she felt in her belly.

She forced herself out of the car. As she was pushing the door she heard a familiar voice. Janelle turned.

Chapter 2

"You're here early too," Reece said, a grin on his lips.

Janelle swallowed hard. The man was a dream. Smooth, cocoa skin, big, brown eyes. There was obvious muscle underneath the clothing. His smile however was the real highlight. He had perfect teeth that seemed to shine and make her melt at the same time.

"I like to be on time."

"Me too," Reece said with a chuckle. He pulled the door open for her, "After you."

The coffee shop was filled with the aroma of brewing coffee beans and sweets. They ordered big cups of coffee before finding seats by a large picture window. Janelle couldn't help the nervousness she now felt. It was different being in the studio where she felt she was in control. Here, it was different.

"So," Reece said breaking the silence, "I got you something."

Janelle raised an eyebrow. "Really now? What did you get me?"

Reece dug into the bag that had been slung over his shoulder. He pulled out a package, wrapped in brown wrapper. She took it from him slowly. He smiled.

"Go ahead, open it. I think you'll like it."

Janelle peeled back the paper slowly. Beneath, she could just make out the words on the cover. She laughed as she pulled the paper off a little more quickly, revealing the thick book underneath.

"History of the World," she said with a shake of her head, a smile on her lips.

"Yeah, you said your copy was falling apart. I figured I'd go pick one up for you. It's a thank you, for getting me on the show."

"Well, thank you. I'm actually really excited about this! Mulder has been scratching at my old one for far too long."

Reece raised an eyebrow. "Mulder? As in the X-Files character?"

Janelle laughed. "Oh, Mulder's my cat. I have a thing for science fiction," she said, trying to keep the embarrassment off of her face. "I know, that's childish..."

"No," Reece said, shaking his head, "that's not childish at all. I love science fiction too. You know, you're too hard on yourself and the things you like."

"You think so?"

"Yeah. I mean, you're a great producer. You're into things like history and science fiction. You have a great laugh. I think everything about you makes you unique."

"Yeah," Janelle said with a scoff, "too unique. Most men can't handle any of that."

"Well," Reece said with a chuckle, "I'm not most men."

Janelle could feel herself becoming embarrassed all over again. She didn't know what Reece's angle was, but he was having an effect on her that she hadn't experienced in a long time. He must have seen her getting uncomfortable, because he quickly changed the subject.

"What's your favorite chapter in the book?"

Janelle smiled. She was glad that Reece quickly changed the

subject. It was nice that he could see her struggling with the attention and go in a different direction. The only problem was that it made her want him even more.

They spent the rest of their time talking about their favorite parts of history. Janelle was amazed with his knowledge, the way he could recall dates off of the top of his head. She was impressed. By the time Janelle glanced at her watch, it was after nine.

"Wow! I didn't realize how late it was," she said as she took another sip out of her second cup of coffee. "I should get going. There's a lot to do on the show tomorrow."

"I should get going too I suppose," Reece said reluctantly. "Can we do this again?"

Janelle bit her lip. "I don't know if we should."

"It's just coffee."

She grinned. "Okay fine. You've convinced me," she said with a chuckle. "This was fun."

They walked out of the coffee shop together. The night air had turned chilly, autumn was finally settling in. He walked her to her car. As she started it, he waved, a smile on his face. Janelle felt a familiar throbbing that made her shake her head. She had to get out of there.

The drive back home, she kept a smile plastered to her face. He was more than she thought he'd be. Funny, smart, sexy, he was a package. She sighed. Too bad dating him now would be the end to her show. That, she couldn't have. Not when the show had been her dream for so long.

Janelle walked into her empty apartment. She didn't mind being alone, but the older she got, the more it weighed on her. There had never really been a man that could catch her attention. Or one that wasn't intimidated by her success. Reece didn't fall into either of those categories.

"Come on, Mulder," she said, scooping up her cat, "it's time for bed. We have a busy day tomorrow."

*****

Reece watched Janelle drive away. She had been the first woman in a long time to peak his interest. The woman was successful, smart, down to earth. He could already feel himself developing feelings for her. He wanted her.

When she was just a dot on the horizon, Reece rounded the building. His car was parked on the other side, his real car. It was a sleek, black BMW, newly purchased. He slipped behind the wheel before he started off for home in the opposite direction.

It took a while to get there from the neighborhood where they met. Reece had a secret. He wasn't just an ordinary man. Although he did love art, he didn't own a gallery or paint expect in his spare time. He pulled up inside of his garage, the two story house looming beside it.

Reece parked the car next to two others before he hopped out. For the show, he'd rented a place that wasn't too far from the studio. It was over sized; six bedrooms, five bathrooms, an entertainment room, a basketball court out back, a pool and Jacuzzi. He would have gone for something smaller, but he still had business deals to make, clients to entertain when he wasn't at the studio.

He walked through the front door and sighed. Another empty house. The bigger they were, the more he was reminded that he still didn't have anyone. That was heartbreaking and disappointing. Reece had tried to date, tried to give women a chance, but it never worked out. They didn't want him for him. The money was always the most enticing thing about him in their eyes.

Reece wasn't sure how he'd come up with the idea. He thought perhaps it might have been Daphne, his little sister's idea. She'd once told him that the money would always bring the thirsty women, the ones who tried to get pregnant just to hold on to him and his cash. Daphne believed that without the money, he'd find the perfect woman.

The man grinned as he picked up the mail from the entrance hallway and flipped through it. Janelle wasn't like that. She was sweet and obviously wasn't used to dating by the way she'd acted at the coffee shop. He wanted to ask her on an actual date, but he could tell by the hesitation in her eyes that she probably would turn him down.

That thought brought a frown to his face as he tossed the mail down. He had a business meeting in the morning, then it would be back to the studio for more filming. Reece flipped on the light in his bedroom before he began to slip out of his clothes. The master suite was huge and filled with antique mahogany furniture and a large king sized bed that seemed to take up a lot of space, but still a lot more remained. The colors were all warm, chocolate browns and forest greens, his favorite colors. He crossed the room to the bathroom.

It was too bad that he had to vote Janelle off. He liked her, she seemed to like him too. He turned on the bathroom light before flipping on the shower. The warm spray quickly steamed up the large bathroom. The shower stood separately from the tub. That was big, round and deep with jets. He stepped into the shower before closing the glass door behind him.

The day had a been a long one. He thought back to the other contestants. They'd been the reason that he'd signed up for the show, but he couldn't really think of one of them that had caught his attention. All he could think about was Janelle's nervous voice saying the first thing that came to her mind. Honest. That's what she was, Reece thought as he rinsed soap off of his brown skin.

He stepped out before wrapping a thick, green towel around his body. Stepping back into his bedroom, he rooted around in his drawers to find a pair of pajama bottoms. The house was pleasantly warm from the heat, but he still shivered as he slipped into the pants.

Reece sighed as he climbed into bed. As he slipped beneath the blanket, he couldn't help but see Janelle's smile. He imagined touching her face, kissing her lips. The thought brought a smile to his face. What would it be like, he wondered, to sleep beside her? To have someone to wrap his arms around at night? The woman had gotten inside his head without even trying.

As Reece tried to force himself to go to sleep, he wondered if Janelle felt anything too? It had only been one day that they'd spent together, but Reece had felt more at home with her than the society sharks he'd grown accustomed to being around. Maybe things would change, he thought. Reece knew one thing for sure, he wanted to see where things could go.

*****

Janelle was in a panic. She ran around her apartment, rooting through her closet for something different to wear. Usually, she didn't much care what she wore, what her hair and makeup looked like. Her abilities had taken her as far as she'd gotten, not her looks.

That morning however, she couldn't get Reece out of her mind. She wanted to look nice, wanted to wow him. Her heart thudded in her chest. She knew it was foolish, stupid really to have a crush on a contestant on a dating show. Still, she couldn't stop the fluttering she felt in her belly every time she thought about him.

Since the day promised to be warm and Janelle had to be on TV again, she settled on a yellow sun dress. It stopped just above her knees and had spaghetti straps. She grabbed a pair of red flats, slipped them on before she headed to the bathroom to fix her hair and makeup.

Janelle reached for her contact case. "Shit!"

The woman watched one of her contacts pop out of the case. It rolled down the sink as she watched on in horror. Janelle could feel her blood pressure rising. Why this morning? She always wore her contacts at work, had for years. Even if they made her eyes itch and annoyed her to put them in, they'd been a necessary evil in her life.

Reluctantly, she reached into the medicine cabinet. The glasses on the top shelf stared back at her menacingly. Janelle sighed, slumped her shoulders as she grabbed them.

She slipped the square frames on her face before she looked at herself in the mirror.

Janelle groaned. "I look like I'm back in middle school!"

Mulder meowed as he circled her ankles. Even his purring, which usually reassured her, didn't help. She didn't like the reflection staring back at her, not today.

"Don't try to make me feel better," she mumbled to Mulder. "I haven't worn glasses in years."

Janelle's phone rang, making her jump. She walked out of the bathroom to the kitchen counter where it lay buzzing and ringing away. Looking at the number, she knew who it was instantly.

"Excuse me, but if I may ask. Where the hell are you?"

"I'm on my way Clark."

"The other contestants are already here. We only have so long to shoot today. There's a lot of editing to be-"

"I'm on my way!"

"Don't get snippy with me girl. Hurry up!"

Janelle sighed as she hung up the phone. Bossy Clark as usual. The man loved his schedules. She wandered back into the bathroom. There was nothing that she could do about the glasses right now, they'd have to do.

Quickly, Janelle brushed out and flat ironed her black hair so that it was straight for once. She pushed a red flower into her hair when she was done. The woman kept her make up light, she didn't want to look like some of the other women who seemed to put the entire makeup aisle on their faces. All it would do is irritate and frustrate her. When she was done, she leaned back to gaze at her reflection.

Janelle smiled. She looked different than her normal self. Usually, a swipe of lipstick, a bun and jeans and a tee were her usual wear. This was different and not bad. She could hear her phone ringing again. Janelle rolled her eyes.

Moving quicker now, she dumped her things into her bag before she grabbed her purse and car keys. The sun was already shining brilliantly when she stepped outside. It was enough to almost make her want to skip work and head to the park to daydream at the water. Her phone ringing for the third time that morning told her that wasn't going to happen. Janelle knew for a fact that Clark would kill her. Besides, with as much work as they had to do, it would be impossible.

Janelle pulled up to the studio a little after ten. When she stepped inside, the contestants were already heading out to the stage. Clark waved her over quickly. He looked impeccable in a coal, gray suit, his blond hair neat, every strand in place.

"What took you so long?" He raised an eyebrow as he looked her up and down. "Never mind," he said with a grin.

Janelle swatted at him. "Shut up!" She said between clenched teeth. "I'm still on TV, remember? I can't exactly do the whole t-shirt and jeans thing."

"Whatever you say," Clark said with a grin.

Janelle rolled her eyes before he pushed her towards the stage. The other women had settled down in their chairs and were chatting quietly before they brought Reece out. She could feel the nervous excitement run though the group. It was kind of fun, she had to admit.

"Let's bring out our bachelor!" Clark was announcing, his brilliant smile shining.

Janelle could hear Reece taking a seat. Her heart starting thudding against her chest quickly. The woman bit her lip. Why was she having that reaction? She liked him sure, but it was just a crush. Right?

"Okay Reece. You can start asking these lovely ladies your questions!"

Unlike the first time, Janelle actually paid attention to what Reece was saying this time. His rich, deep voice made her want to shiver. When it was her turn, she could almost hear the smile on his lips.

"Tara, why don't you tell me some of your hobbies?"

Janelle grinned. "I don't have very many hobbies. I like to read. Staying healthy is kind of important to me so I like jogging. Mostly, I enjoy drawing. I've been doing that for a while, but I've never showed anyone."

"Wow, really? What do you draw?"

"Just about everything I suppose. People are my favorite

subjects though."

"That's really interesting," Reece said.

"Okay, let's move on to our next contestant," Clark was saying.

Janelle couldn't wipe the smile off of her face. The longer the show went on, the more she realized just how much they had in common. They both liked the same kinds of food, the same movies, they loved the same cities. It was odd to be so compatible with someone.

In the back of her mind, Janelle wished that she could stay a little longer. She didn't want to be off of the show so soon, not when it was so fun getting to know Reece. Still, she knew that it had to be done. It was her show after all. The more she was sitting on the stage, the less time she had to make sure that the show ran smoothly.

"Okay, Reece. You've gotten to talk to all of our contestants. Now, it's time for you to tell us who you'll be eliminating tonight?"

"Well," Reece said slowly, "I had a good time, talking to all of you. There is one person who stands out in my mind so far.

I'm going to have to say goodbye to Tara. Sorry Tara."

Janelle nodded. "I enjoyed my time here," she said with a smile.

The woman nodded as she waved and walked off of the stage. She had been expecting it, but it had still been unpleasant. The thought of him sitting up there, chatting with the other women was a little annoying, but it had to be done. She walked back towards her office.

Mya was already glancing at the tapes, making notes. She glanced up when Janelle walked in then returned to work. Quickly, the woman did a double take.

"Well, look at you," Mya said with a grin.

"Don't start," Janelle said as she took a seat and picked up a headset. "Don't even start."

Mya grinned. "Fine. I won't say anything."

They worked in silence, but every once in a while she would catch Mya glancing at her. Janelle glared as she tried to work. They were driving her crazy. She knew that tomorrow she'd be back to her jeans and tees. Janelle wasn't used to all of the attention and it was starting to irritate her.

"What do you think?" Mya asked as the filming finished up.

"It's not bad. Get everyone back for these parts, here and here," she said pointing. "The audio faded out for a minute. Can you check on that?"

"Sure thing. I'll have everyone reset in ten?"

Janelle nodded. "Sounds good."

"Janelle," Clark said as he stuck his head inside of the door, "Reece wants to speak with you."

"Okay. I'll head there now. We're resetting in ten."

"Roger, Captain," Clark said before he disappeared.

"I'll be back," Janelle called as she left out of the office.

The nervousness was back as she headed towards Reece's dressing room. She knocked on the door lightly before his filtered 'come in' came through the door. Janelle pushed the door open and stepped inside. She paused.

Reece was standing there, without his shirt on. She felt her face get hot. The muscles that she'd suspected were beneath his clothes were enticing. He began to button up the new shirt quickly.

"Sorry about that. I thought I'd try this one. One of your interns said the other one was too dark."

Janelle nodded dumbly. "Yeah, you look good. It! It looks good. I like the...shirt," she cleared her throat. "You wanted to talk to me?"

Reece was grinning. "Yeah. I wanted to know if you would maybe want to get together. Catch dinner? I feel like I owe you something nice after having to eliminate you."

She laughed. "Oh, really now?" Janelle shook her head. "Well, I wish I could. I don't really have the funds at the moment...," she said slowly.

"That's okay. I don't want to pressure you."

"If you want though," she said, pushing herself to speak up, "we could order take in, sit on my couch and watch TV with Mulder."

Reece's grin spread. "That sounds good."

"Good. I'll see you tonight. Oh, here's my address, I should probably give you that," she mumbled as she pulled a piece of paper out and began to scribble it down. When she was done, she handed it to him, that old nervousness back once again.

He gazed at the paper for a minute. "Is eight okay?"

She smiled. "Eight is fine."

"Can I bring anything?"

"Wine would not be turned down," she said with a laugh. "Oh, I have to get back to work. We're resetting in ten, well seven now. Okay?"

"Sounds good. I'll see you out there."

Janelle couldn't seem to stop the grin that had taken up permanent residence on her lips. She stepped out of his dressing room before she closed the door behind herself. Janelle shook her head. She didn't know what she was thinking, but it had almost been an impulse to invite him over. She was glad that she had.

Chapter 3

Janelle had never been especially good at social interaction. When it came to her work, she knew what she needed and what needed to be done. Her confidence in her job was part of the reason she had the position she did now. Outside of that, she generally didn't know what to say. Socially awkward. That was how Clark often described her. While other people were partying, she was making friends with the resident cat. Animals had always been kinder to her than humans.

So, she couldn't understand why talking to Reece, while sometimes nerve wracking, could be so easy. She pushed herself out of her seat as they began to reset. Walking onto the set, she slipped on her headset. Now, she could see both the contestants and Reece. As she came into view, he winked at her before he grinned.

Stop it, heart!

Janelle waved back to him lightly before she focused her attention on the show. It was going smoothly, very smoothly. Despite their upset the first day of shooting, it looked like the show was actually going to go well without too many problems. She folded her arms as she watched, a smile on her face. Her first successful show. It would be the validation that she so desperately needed in her career.

Mya bumped her arm. "Quit smiling at the bachelor."

"I wasn't!"

A few people turned to look at her. Janelle could feel her face get hot. She glared at Mya who was obviously stifling a laugh behind her stony exterior.

"I could fire you, you know?" Janelle said as she glared.

"Please, what would you do without me?"

"Do your job!" Janelle scolded before they turned their attention back to the set.

It was a productive afternoon. Janelle was happy with the way the show was coming along, but she still didn't seem to be able to stop gazing at Reece. Every time he caught her eye, there was a little spark of electricity that traveled up her spine. She couldn't stop smiling at him.

"That's it for the day," she called after their last take. "Good job everyone! Be back here tomorrow bright and early to film the next episode."

Janelle watched the contestants file off of the stage. First the women, then Reece. They had to keep them separate to maintain the integrity of the show. Once the stage was clear, Janelle took time to talk to Mya before she went in search of Reece. She had a few points to go over with him, then edit the tapes with Mya. She couldn't wait to get home. The thought of him being at her place made her nervous, but she couldn't wait to see him without everyone else around.

She walked down the hall saying goodnight to the people who were leaving early. When she turned down Reece's hallway, she saw something that made her stop in her tracks. A woman, Patricia she thought she remembered the woman's name being, was standing at Reece's door, fiddling with it. The woman was concentrating on opening the door so hard, that she didn't hear Janelle swiftly approaching her.

"What do you think you're doing?"

The woman jumped. She was short, no more than five feet with light brown skin and big, brown eyes. Her chestnut colored hair was long. The woman had a small figure, but was curvy in the right places. Janelle raised an eyebrow as the woman turned around, something metal in her hand.

"What are you doing?" Janelle asked again, this time anger filtering into her voice.

"I -I was just..."

"Trying to see Reece?" Janelle added for her. "No one is allowed to see the bachelor before the finale."

"I know," the woman said, her voice almost whiny. "I just wanted-"

Janelle narrowed her eyes. "There is no 'I just wanted' Patricia. You are *not* allowed to see the bachelor before the finale, do I make myself clear?"

Patricia's nice demeanor seemed to quickly fade. "Yeah."

"I'm serious," Janelle said taking a step closer. "If I catch you doing anything like this again, I'm canceling your contract. You'll go home with nothing."

"Look," Patricia said as she propped her hands on her hips. "It's already very obvious that he likes me. I just wanted to say hi to him."

"Go," Janelle said pointing down the hallway, "Now."

Patrica didn't argue, but the expression on her face wasn't the friendliest. She turned on her heels, tossed her hair before she was down the hall, swaying her hips as she went. Janelle scoffed.

"This show seems to bring out the craziest people," she mumbled, shaking her head before she knocked on Reece's door.

One thing was for sure, she'd have to keep a closer eye on the contestants. Janelle couldn't believe that woman. He obviously liked her? She barely remembered the woman's answers and she'd sat right beside her. Janelle highly doubted that Reece had a thing for her.

Maybe he does. You weren't exactly paying attention to the other women, she thought to herself as she heard the dressing room door unlock. Reece was standing there, a smile on his face.

"I think we said eight," he teased.

Janelle laughed. "I'm aware. I just wanted to talk to you about the show before you leave."

"Come on in," he said holding open the door to his dressing room.

Janelle stepped inside. She wondered if she'd ever get enough of walking into that room? A part of her didn't think she would. They discussed the show for a little while before Janelle excused herself.

"More editing. A producer's work is never done," she said as she stood up from the chair she'd been sitting in.

"I'm sure you'll make the show amazing. I'll see you tonight," he said as he let her out.

Janelle grinned as she started to walk away.

"Oh, Janelle?" Reece called.

"Yes?"

"I love your glasses. You look really nice today."

Janelle could feel the heat spread through her body to her

face. She knew that big, stupid grin was on her face again, but there was no wiping it off. She was so stumped that she didn't know how to respond. Instead, she nodded her head and walked away quickly, the sound of her footsteps echoing in the hallway as she retreated. Janelle refused to even turn around. She had a suspicion that Reece would still be smiling at her brilliantly.

*****

Janelle had slipped out of the dress some time ago. She traded it in for a pair of comfortable yoga pants and a black tank top. Her hair was back in its usual bun, but the glasses were still perched on her nose. She didn't feel so self-conscious about them anymore. Being teased about them when she was younger had been wiped out by Reece's warm eyes and silken words.

A knock on the door jolted her out of her thoughts. Nervous excitement flooded her stomach. She took a deep breath before she opened the door. Reece stood there looking amazing as usual. He wore dark blue jeans, a black t-shirt and sneakers. The man smiled as he held up the bottle of wine that he'd promised to bring.

"I hope you like red," he said.

"Love it," she said as she stepped aside. "Come on in."

Once he was inside, he seemed to gaze around her place in approval. Janelle went to fetch the takeout menus that she kept stashed in the drawer beside her stove. When she turned around, Reece was there.

"Jesus!" She said laughing nervously. "You scared me."

"Sorry about that. You have a *lot* of takeout menu's," he said raising an eyebrow.

"Yeah," she said sheepishly, "I don't really get to cook much. I'm always working," she mumbled to herself. "Besides, there's variety here! Chinese, Thai, Soul Food, healthy stuff, there's even Greek. Oh and Italian of course."

"I have a better idea."

"Oh?" Janelle asked raising an eyebrow.

"Why don't you let me cook something for you? While I'm cooking, you can sit on the counter and critique me. With wine of course."

Janelle laughed. "Are you sure?"

"Yeah, it'll give me a chance to show off. Bragging rights are important," he said with a wink.

"Well, good luck to you in your endeavors Mr. James, but I am one picky eater. That and my cabinets are pretty bare?"

"I see that," Reece mumbled as he opened the refrigerator and then the cabinets.

"Shut up!" Janelle laughed. "Work, remember?"

Reece shook his head. "Still girl, how do you live?"

"Leave me alone!" She said swatting at him.

Reece chuckled. "Fine. Let's go to the store first."

"Limited funds, remember?"

"I said I was cooking, right? Of course I have to get the ingredients as well, let's go."

"Oh," Janelle protested as he took her by the hand, "I'm a mess!"

"You look good," he reassured her with a grin.

Janelle wasn't sure how much more of Reece she could take. The man was doing things to her that didn't even require him touching her. She nodded her head as she slipped on a pair of sneakers and locked up her place.

They traveled to the grocery store near her house. Reece wanted her to pick out what she wanted to eat, but she insisted that was cheating. He laughed as they browsed the aisle until he settled on what he wanted to make her.

"You're seriously going to let me throw away food if you don't like what I make?" He asked, pushing the cart.

"Yes. Well, no," she laughed. "I would tell you if I totally hated the food you bought. I don't know what you're going to make, but it looks good already."

"Damn straight it looks good. I'm going to blow you away with this meal."

Janelle rolled her eyes. "You doing a *whole* lot of hyping there."

"Fine," he laughed. "I'll shut up and put up."

When they were back at Janelle's house again, Reece opened the bottle of wine for her. He poured her out a glass before he poured himself one too. She perched herself on her counter and watched him pull out pots and pans.

Janelle sipped her wine as she watched him work. He had pulled out pasta, but he hadn't bought sauce at the store. There was steak out, two big nice cuts that looked beautiful before he'd even touched them. On the counter, there was shrimp.

"Where's the sauce?" She asked.

"Shh, you're judging. You can't be asking questions."

Janelle laughed. "So, I'm the judge now?"

"Yes, ma'am."

"Fine," she said taking a big sip of her wine. "Here we have Reece James. I don't know what that guy's thinking? He has absolutely no sauce for his pasta."

"Wrong!"

"What do you mean wrong?" Janelle asked, pretending to

glare. "I can see just fine."

"Can you?" He asked, pushing up her glasses.

Janelle laughed before she shook her head. "Fine, I'll be quiet and let you work."

The woman watched him as he cooked up the steak and shrimp, the pasta boiling on the back burner. When it was all done and sitting on their plates, he began to mix flour, milk and butter in a sauce pan. She watched him season it before he swirled the spoon a few more times and lifted it to Janelle's lips. She tasted it tentatively.

"Oh my God," she said, eyelids fluttering. "That's just heavenly."

"I told you," he said.

Janelle could tell he was proud of himself as he began to pour the sauce over their food. They took their food into the living room where Janelle turned on the TV. They settled for a romantic comedy Janelle had seen multiple times, but still enjoyed. She ate her food slowly, trying not to look like a slob.

"Are you going to only take little bites out of that all night? Or are you going to eat it?"

Janelle laughed. "I was being polite!"

"Girl, if you don't dig into that food."

Janelle shrugged. Living by herself, she'd become used to eating the way she pleased. As she really began to dig into her meal, she glanced out of the corner of her eye. Reece grinned before he turned back to the TV. *He's so cute.*

They sat together long after their plates were cleared and the dishwasher was running. Janelle rubbed her feet lightly. They were sore from running all over the studio all day in the little flats. Without warning, Reece grabbed her feet and put them on his lap. He began to rub them without a word.

"Y-you don't have to do that."

"Shh," he put a finger up to his lips, "the movie."

Janelle grinned as she turned her attention back to the screen. She wasn't really looking at it though. Instead, she found her eyes closing at intervals, the feeling of Reece rubbing her feet making her moan softly. He poured her another glass of wine, which she happily accepted.

"Are you trying to get me drunk?" She teased.

Reece laughed. "I don't think I need to with the way you're moaning over there."

Janelle stifled a laugh. "I'm glad you came over."

"Me too," he said with a grin. Reece glanced at his watch. "It's past mid-night," he groaned.

"You've had too much wine to drive home, haven't you?"

Reece nodded slowly. "I'm pretty sure I shouldn't be behind the wheel."

"Well," Janelle said standing up and extending a hand, "you can sleep with me tonight. No funny business."

Reece held up his hands. "Yes, ma'am. I wouldn't dream of it."

"That's disappointing," she mumbled.

"What was that?"

"Nothing!" Janelle chimed up quickly. "Come on."

She turned off the TV before she led him upstairs to her

bedroom. The bed was still neatly made, her dress lying on top of it. She picked it up and slipped it onto the hanger before she stuck it inside of her closet. When she turned around, Reece had slipped out of his shirt and jeans, only his blue boxers were left. She swallowed.

"I can't sleep in jeans," he explained quickly. "I'm way too old for that," he said with a chuckle.

Janelle nodded, but she was at a lost for words. Instead, she slipped her bra off before she slid into bed next to him. Reaching over, she clicked off the light after she'd set her alarm. Janelle pulled the blankets up to her chin.

"Reece?" She said into the darkness of the room.

"Yeah?" He called back.

Janelle could feel the heat from his body beside her. "What are we doing? You have to pick one of those women from the show."

"I know."

"So, what are we doing?"

"We're..." he drifted off, not quite sure how to answer that question himself.

Janelle felt his hand reach over towards her. She could tell that he was hesitating, so was she. Still, she found herself slipping her hand inside of his. Her vision had adjusted to the relative darkness, the only light from the street light outside of her window, filtering through the blinds. Janelle could just make him out, gazing at her.

"What?" She asked softly.

Without warning, Reece slid closer. He captured her mouth in his. Janelle's brain protested, they couldn't do this! Not with the show. Still, she didn't stop. Instead, her mouth was just as eager and hungry as his. Reece propped himself up and rolled on top of her. She moaned.

Janelle could feel his warm skin pressing against hers. His hands cradled her face. She gasped against his mouth. Reece's hands began to slip downward as her heart pounded in her chest. She didn't know if it was the wine or the effect he was having on her, but her heart had began to speed up in her chest.

"Reece," she mumbled against his lips.

The man was much too preoccupied with her mouth. His tongue slipped into her mouth, sought out hers until he was teasing her tongue with quick flicks and languid strokes. She lost her breath, a shiver passing through her body.

"Shit," she said softly as he pulled back and began to leave kisses on her neck.

Reece's mouth seemed to find the most sensitive spots on her neck. His lips kissed softly, his tongue applied pressure, his teeth made her back arch up from the mattress. Her hands curled around his strong arms as he teased and tasted every inch of her. Slowly, he moved downward.

"Reece," she called softly, "I'm not ready to have sex. I haven't in a while. And I promised myself that I wouldn't again until I really cared about someone..." she trailed off.

He gazed up at her. "I don't want to have sex with you yet either," he said with a grin. "I just want this," he said as he kissed her collarbone. "Is this okay?"

Janelle nodded quickly. "That's more than fine. That-that's

amazing," she moaned.

Reece made his way down her body. First his lips, then his tongue, then teeth. Every inch of her skin felt electrified. His hands pushed up her shirt as he gazed at her as if checking to make sure it was okay. Janelle nodded once more and Reece quickly got rid of the shirt altogether. His mouth kissed her breasts. Janelle shuddered. Reece's tongue darted out over her breasts. She moaned deeply, her pussy twitching.

He kept traveling down. Reece left kisses on her belly, on her inner thighs. He stayed there a while, between her legs, teasing her. Janelle was biting her lip as she moaned. She almost wanted to yell at him, tell him to stop driving her crazy. Just when she was on the verge of losing her mind, his fingers gripped the hem of her shorts and panties.

Janelle lifted her hips as he began to slide them down. The fabric slid across her skin slowly. When he pulled them off, he threw them to the floor. Janelle closed her legs tightly. She felt the shyness coming back, making her close herself up. Reece however didn't rush her. He kissed her legs, ran fingers over her skin as he gazed up at her, a small grin on his lips.

Without realizing it, Janelle felt her legs falling open. Reece ran a finger over her inner thigh making her shiver. His fingernails raked over her skin making her writhe in the bed. She gasped as he leaned forward.

Reece took his time. His fingers ran over her slit. She knew they would brush through her wetness. Janelle could feel his fingers at her entrance, knew that he wanted to plunge them inside of her. Instead, he leaned forward, ran his tongue over her clit in one, quick motion.

Janelle gasped. She could feel her pussy throbbing, twitching. Biting her lip, she gazed down at him. He seemed amused by her reaction as he went back to running his tongue over her clit. Reece switched from lazy, slow licks to hungry, desperate licking. Janelle's back arched.

The woman could feel her body getting close. Her toes curled. Her fingers clutched the covers as she moaned loudly, uninhibited for the first time in a long time. Janelle's eyes were closed tightly, her mind concentrating on the feeling of his tongue slipping and sliding over her clit.

"Fuck!"
Janelle cried out as he slipped a finger inside of her. She moaned, twisted her hips to capture the sensation of

something being inside of her pussy. Reece quickly added another finger. Janelle was moaning, gasping as he began to work his fingers in and out of her quickly. His fingers fucked her the same way his mouth worked on her pussy. Janelle was in ecstasy.

Reece seemed to enjoy himself as his fingers thrust inside of her. He crooked his fingers. Janelle's eyes flew open as she gasped. He was rubbing her g-spot, running his fingers over it easily as she moaned and ground her hips in circles. Janelle found her hands reached up for her breasts. She gripped both of them, pulled and tweaked her nipples as she bit her lip. Janelle let out a deep moan as the orgasm took over her. Her pussy clenched his fingers tightly as her stomach tightened. When she opened her eyes, Reece was grinning at her.

"Don't grin at me like that," she said trying to catch her breath.

"Why not?" He teased.

Janelle rolled her eyes. "I guess it's your turn," she said as she started to shift.

Reece grabbed her arm before he pushed her back down on her pillow. He climbed back beside her before pulling the blanket over both of them. Sighing, he wrapped an arm around her before pulling her closer to him. In the darkness, Janelle smiled.

Chapter 4

Reece was over the show. He didn't want the other two women. Not when he could have Janelle. She was perfect. The more time he spent around her, the more he felt himself falling for her. He couldn't stop thinking about her. The way her back arched, the way her mouth felt on his, the curves of her body, the softness of her skin...

The man opened the front door to his house. A blur of color bounded up to him before arms were thrown around his neck. When he looked down, he saw a short woman in a jogging outfit and sneakers. Her brown skin was smooth. When she pulled away from Reece, there was a big smile on her face.

"Daphne," Reece said in surprise. "What are you doing here?"

"I was in town, so I thought that I'd visit. Besides, tomorrow is the finale of the show right? I heard it's a live show."

"And?"

"And," Daphne said with her hands on her hips and her no nonsense attitude firmly in place. "I want to be there! I've been keeping up with the show!" She said excitedly.

Reece sighed. "I don't know if I even *want* to do the show anymore," he admitted as he closed the garage door.

Daphne raised an eyebrow. "Why not? I thought this was your brilliant idea to find true love or something like that."

"It *was*, but...."

"But what?"

Reece shrugged. "I think I already found it."

Daphne clapped excitedly. "Where did you meet her?"

"On the show, surprisingly," Reece said with a laugh as he headed to the kitchen with Daphne in tow. "She's actually the producer of the show."

"Have you told her?"

"Told her what," Reece asked as he dug around in the fridge.

"Duh! That you love her. Pay attention."

"Woah, I don't know if it's love..."

Daphne crossed her arms over her chest. "I don't think you've seen your face when you talk about her. You clearly love her."

Reece didn't respond as he pulled out eggs and bacon. He cracked the eggs in a bowl before glancing at his phone. There wasn't that much time left to get to the studio on time, so he'd have to hurry. He was trying to avoid Daphne's glare as he whisked the eggs.

Finally Daphne sighed. "You can deny it all you want to, but you love her. And if she's amazing enough to catch your picky attention, I would tell her. Before someone else does," she called as she walked toward the entrance of the kitchen.

"Where are you going?" Reece called.

"I'm going on my run, then I'm coming back to change for the show!"

Reece heard the front door close behind her. He sighed. She was nosy, but she wasn't wrong. Reece loved being around Janelle, he wanted to ask her out. The last time he'd tried, she'd become nervous and timid. Still, he wanted her. More than he'd ever wanted anyone.

He finished his breakfast before getting dressed for the show.

His heart pounded in his chest during the entire drive. What he had in mind could have some consequences, but he knew he had to do it. Reece smiled. The small bit of nervousness that dwelled within his belly wasn't enough to keep him from Janelle.

*****

Janelle felt life falling into a routine. She'd wake up, work on the show, meet up with Reece after. Sometimes they'd grab coffee or watch a movie together, other times he'd wrap her up in his arms as they watched a movie together in her bed. Janelle had never had so much fun around someone. She'd become completely comfortable with Reece.

Smiling, she walked through the studio, clipboard in hand. She glanced at the stage where they were about to shoot one of the final scenes. Reece looked amazing as usual; a purple, striped button down, black slacks and a wide grin. When she caught his eye, he winked at her before chuckling. Janelle felt her stomach flutter nervously.

"There you go again," Clark said with a laugh as he approached her. "You really have a thing for him, don't you?"

Janelle shook her head quickly. "We're just friends."

"Sure," Clark said with a big grin on his lips. "Sure you are."

"Would you stop that?" Janelle asked with a scowl, holding her head up higher. "Besides, it wouldn't matter. He has to pick one of those two, remember?"

Clark placed a hand on her shoulder. "I'm sorry. You guys really did seem to be alike."

You have no idea, Janelle thought. They really were very compatible, but she knew it couldn't happen. Not to mention the fact that she still wasn't sure if she was ready to date. Hanging out with Reece was one thing, complicating it with a relationship was a completely different thing entirely.

Janelle bit her lip. "Who do you think he'll pick?"

Clark laughed at this. "Not that crazy ass Patricia. At least I hope not. She stalked me around all morning asking who he was going to choose," Clark shook his head. "She definitely has a few screws loose."

She laughed. "Don't I know it. I caught her trying to break into his dressing room last week."

"Seriously?"

"Oh yeah," Janelle said. "Look, can't you tell I've pissed her off? She's been staring daggers at me since I ran her off from his door."

Clark glanced over at Patricia. He stifled a laugh. "We might need security after he chooses."

"Already covered," Janelle pointed over to the right to two men standing in the shadows.

"Nicely done, Peters," Clark said as he looked back at her. "Ready to get this freak show started?"

Janelle shook her head. "It's not a freak show, but yes. We should start soon. Is the audience in place?"

"They're a little rowdy, but it looks like a full house. Which is good news. Ratings are going to be through the roof. How does it feel to produce your first successful show?" Clark asked.

Bittersweet. That was what Janelle wanted to say. She loved the fact that her show was actually off the ground and doing well, but then there was Reece. She almost couldn't take the thought of him choosing another woman. Still, she smiled.

"It feels good. I'm doing what I love," she said to Clark.

The man obviously saw something in her eyes, but he closed his mouth right after he opened it. Janelle was happy that he did. She didn't want to explain about Reece. The thought of it would hurt too much if she had to say anything out loud.

"You look really nice today," Clark said instead. "It's nice to see you come out of your shell."

Janelle laughed. "Thanks. I didn't want to look tore up in front of the audience," she said, her face growing hot.

That had been part of the reason, but not all of it. When she slipped into the little black dress that barely brushed her knees, she'd been thinking about Reece. If it was the last time she was going to see him, she wanted him to have good memories. The dress dipped lower in the front, hinting at cleavage. She wore heels too, tall, black ones that made her legs look amazing, as Mya had said. Her hair as well was courtesy of Mya. Long, wavy, beautiful. Her glasses were perched on her nose. She felt amazing, but it still felt sad. After today, Reece would have a new woman in his life. No time for her.

"We should get going," she said suddenly, refusing to let her emotions screw up the ending of her show.

"Let's do it!" Clark said excitedly.

"Quiet on the set!" Janelle called as the quiet signs lit up.

The crowd behind her quieted down. She glanced at them. Most of them were women, waiting and eager to see who would be leaving with the handsome bachelor. Most of them continued to whisper to one another as they pointed at Reece. Janelle turned her attention back to the stage.

Clark was taking his place in front of the contestants. He adjusted the black, suit jacket he wore as he held a mic up to his lips. Janelle raised her fingers, he nodded. 3...2...1...

The sign lit up for applause and the studio turned into an uproar of cheers and applause. Clark basked in the attention as he waved to the crowd. His mega-watt smile was wide. When the quiet sign lit up once more and the applause had subsided Clark began.

"Ladies and gentlemen, welcome back to *Match Made in*

Heaven. This is the day that everyone's been waiting for. Today, Reece will choose between these two lovely ladies, Patricia and Amber. First, we'll have three more rounds of questions so our bachelor can get one final chance to get to know them. Ready?"

"Ready!" The contestant's voices chimed.

The show started off as usual. Reece asked the women questions and they answered in their sultriest or most giggle filled voices. Janelle lost count of how many times she rolled her eyes before Mya elbowed her. The closer they got to the end of the show, the more the tension in the studio became palpable.

"This is it ladies and gentlemen," Clark said in his deep, mysterious voice as he gazed out into the audience.

Everyone in the audience seemed to be holding their breath. Janelle couldn't help but feel satisfaction at the fact that they looked so excited. Her show had been a hit. Even if she couldn't have Reece.

"Reece," Clark said, turning to the bachelor, "who will you be taking with you today? Patricia or Amber?"

Reece seemed to be contemplating it for a moment. Finally, he stood up from his chair. The man flashed his big smile before he looked at the audience.

"I actually have a confession to make," the man said, prompting the audience to gasp.

Clark looked at Janelle with an uneasy expression. Janelle signaled him to keep going. Whatever Reece was doing, it would more than likely be astronomical for ratings. Clark turned back to Reece.

"Go ahead, Reece. What's on your mind?"

"Well, first of all I'd like to say that I really have enjoyed getting to know all of the contestants. You were all interesting and I really liked hearing your stories. However, I haven't been very honest." Reece took a deep breath. "First of all, I'm not the owner of an art gallery. I'm actually a wall street investor. A billionaire, really," he said, running his hand over the back of his head nervously.

Mya glanced at Janelle. Lost, Janelle could only shrug her shoulders. She had no idea what was going on, but she was intrigued. A billionaire. What was he doing on her show?

"I lied because I got tired of women dating me for my money. So, I decided to get on this show and just get to know you ladies, personally. After all of that, I do have to say that I found who I'm meant to be with," he said with a smile.

"I'm sure our audience would love to know which lady that is?" Clark said with a grin.

Janelle could tell that Clark was soaking in the drama. He loved things like this. However, she had to admit that her heart was beating against her chest wildly. She had no idea what Reece was doing. Everything was out of her control. It was thrilling and new. She was eating it up right along with everyone else.

"Well, Clark," Reece said with a grin, "she's really special. She's smart, funny, awkward and she loves history as much as I do."

When Reece turned towards her, Janelle felt her mouth fall open. She wanted to ask him what he thought he was doing? Her voice was stuck in her throat though. She couldn't think beyond staring at him.

"Janelle, I fell for you the first time we talked. I can't pretend that I don't want you. That I'm not...in love with you. I want more of those late nights on the couch. More of those deep conversations that never end. I love you. Will you go on a *real* date with me tonight?"

Janelle could feel her mouth open and close, but no words were escaping. She glanced at Mya and Clark. Both of them seemed to be shocked too, they were no help. The woman glanced back on the stage at Reece. She wasn't sure if she was ready for that, for anything.

A date. A real date. She let the thought process in her mind. And he loved her. It was much too quick for them to have those kinds of feelings, wasn't it? Still, Janelle couldn't deny that she felt something for him as well.

Janelle slipped the headset off. Slowly, she walked up to the stage. The look on the other two women's faces ranged from disbelief to fury. Janelle could deal with that later, for now she walked up to Reece.

"What do you say?" He said in a low, deep voice.

Janelle nodded slowly. "Okay. A date it is."

Reece leaned down. His lips brushed against hers lightly before he kissed her so deeply that she could feel her knees go weak. Sighing, she leaned against it, taking in the moment without thinking of anything else. Behind her, she could hear Clark speaking and the roar of the audience. They were clapping, stomping, screaming.

"That's *Match Made in Heaven,* ladies and gentlemen. Until next time," Clark called.

The show was over. Janelle pulled back from Reece, her hands placed on his chest. He looked at her with his deep chocolate eyes and she grinned.

"Dinner, tonight?"

"Yes," she said slowly. "You have some explaining to do."

"Quite a bit," he said with a chuckle. "I'll pick you up at seven?"

"Sounds good," Janelle could hear Patricia screaming as she stormed around the screen that had separated her and Reece. "I better go deal with the fallout."

"Sorry," he said looking sheepish. "Let me help."

"What the hell is this?" Patricia asked, her hands propped on her hips. "I spent all of this time on this show for him to choose *you?* This is bullshit!"

Amber peeked around the divider as well. She gave a small wave to Reece. The man grinned as he walked over to both of them.

"Let me guess, you're Amber and you're Patricia?"

Amber nodded as Patricia stopped in her tracks, staring at Reece. Janelle felt her jealously stir. However, she decided to let Reece take the lead, for now anyway. He should apologize to them anyway.

"Amber," he said shaking her hand, "you look amazing. I enjoyed your thoughts and ideas. You're very smart."

Amber was grinning, a slight pink tint on her cheeks. "Thank you. I'm glad I got to meet you," she said with a chuckle. "I'm a bit jealous, but I'm glad that you found someone that makes you happy. Good luck you two. This was fun."

Reece turned to Patricia. She as a bit harder to soothe. The woman kept shooting daggers at Janelle as if she could kill her by evil looks alone. That almost made Janelle want to roll her eyes, but instead she decided to remain the mature adult in the situation.

"This isn't fair!" Patricia was saying, her arms now folded across her chest. "I played this game just like everyone else and made it to this round. You can't do this! We had a connection," she said to Reece. "I'm going to sue the crap out of this show," she said as she jabbed a finger towards Janelle.

"I think I have a solution," Reece was saying as he reached into his back pocket.

Janelle glanced over at him as he wrote out two checks. He gave one to each of the women. Both of their eyes went wide. Amber immediately tucked hers inside of her bra while Patricia glanced between him and the check.

"Of course," Reece said quickly, "the condition to those checks is that neither one of you sues this show or Janelle. Understood?"

Amber nodded quickly. "No problem with me! Thanks!" She gave him a hug before she was off of the stage in a flash.

Patricia sighed. "Fine. I'll take your stupid check," she looked him up and down. "We could have had something special."

"I know it," Reece said, giving her a wink.

The woman grinned before she too left the stage. Janelle let out a deep breath that she'd been holding since the women first walked up to them. Everything seemed to be smoothed over. She turned to Reece, a broad smile on her lips.

"You're amazing," she said.

"Oh, you have no idea," he said as he grabbed her into another deep kiss.

*****

Janelle raced around her apartment. As much as she'd been around Reece in the past few weeks, she felt as if this was different. This was an *actual* date. She hadn't gone on one of those in so long that she'd forgotten what it felt like. Frantically, she texted him as she glanced at the clock. It was already six.

What am I supposed to wear?

Reece texted back promptly. *Something should be arriving*

just about now.

No sooner had she read the text, there was a knock on the door. She walked over, a towel still wrapped around her body as she threw open the door. A man stood there, several boxes in his hands. Janelle signed for them before he was off again. She closed and locked her door.

Janelle opened the big box first. Inside, there was a dress in a pearl pink color. It was long, the front dipped low to show off her cleavage. The back cut down to show off her back. She pulled the dress up to herself and gazed into the mirror.

"Not bad," she mumbled as she moved back and forth.

Janelle made herself focus as she went back for the next box. It held a pair of pearl pink shoes. Another box held a wrap that matched the dress. The last box was jewelry. Sparkling diamonds glittered at her in the form of a necklace, bracelet and earrings. She swallowed thickly. He really was rich.

That made her even more nervous. She wasn't poor herself, but she didn't have billions, that was for sure. She bit her lip. What if she backed out? Just said no? Janelle chided herself. No, she was going to put herself out there for once. Besides, she deserved to be happy.

She carried the boxes up to her room before she dropped the towel. First, she slipped on the lacy white underwear that she'd purchased before she drove home from the studio. The material against her skin felt soft, sexy. She smiled softly at her reflection in the mirror.

Janelle slipped the dress on next. It looked amazing against her brown skin. It showed just enough cleavage to not make her uncomfortable and it was the perfect size. She slipped into the shoes before sliding on the jewelry. It laid against her skin, sparkling and cool.

She walked downstairs to start on her makeup. Janelle kept it simple; mascara, eye shadow and a nude lipstick to compliment the dress. Mya had already helped her curl her hair before she'd left. All she had to do was pin it up. When she was done, she stared at herself and blinked.

"Woah," she whispered, "I look amazing."

Janelle stuck her makeup, money and ID inside of a clutch that had been tucked inside of the dress box. A smile was on her lips. It had been a long time since she felt like this. She glanced at her phone. It was almost seven. Reece was always on time too, all she had to do was wait.

She walked out of the bathroom, shutting the light off as she went. Mulder twisted himself between her ankles as usual as she walked into the living room. Nervousness lay in her stomach. She tried to push it away. She needed this. Besides, she was just as excited as she was nervous.

When she glanced at her phone again, she noticed that Clark and Mya had already texted her twice. She text them back before she sat on a bar stool in the kitchen. Janelle wondered absently where he was going to take her when there was a knock on the door. She jumped.

Quickly, she slid out of her seat and headed over to the door. Taking a deep breath, she steadied herself. She pulled open the door.

Chapter 5

"Wow," Reece said as he gazed at Janelle.

Right away, she felt embarrassed. She hadn't worn clothes like that in a long time, she felt good. It was still kind of odd to be the center of attention though. It was one thing when they were just hanging around her house or lounging at coffee houses, but this was different.

"You look amazing," Reece said as he glanced at her. He shook his head as if trying to think straight. He held out his arm towards her. "Are you ready to go?"

"Yes," she said. She stepped out of the apartment before locking it behind her. "I suppose I'm ready," she said as she took his arm.

"Don't be nervous," he said with a chuckle, just pretend it's like every other time that we've been around each other."

Janelle nodded. She'd been so nervous that she hadn't gotten a good peek at Reece until now. He wore a tailored black suit, red tie and expensive looking black shoes. He'd recently shaved and the smell of his cologne was intoxicating.

Reece helped her slip into the car before he closed her door for her. She folded her hands in her lap as he sat behind the wheel. The car they were in now was different than the one she'd become accustomed to. It was sleek, black and expensive.

"All of this is so...different," she mumbled as they pulled off.

Reece nodded understandingly. "I get it. You knew me as one way for weeks, now I seem completely different. It's hard to get your head around."

Janelle smiled. He was always able to read her so easily. She chuckled, the tension melting away.

"You're right. I mean, we're still the same people."

"Of course. You'll still snore when you sleep and I'll still be an amazing cook."

Janelle rolled her eyes. "Why does mine have to be negative?"

"Shh, I didn't make the rules."

She couldn't stifle her laughter anymore. The woman shook her head as they drove, the conversation becoming easy between the two of them. She glanced at the passing street signs, eager to know where he was taking her.

"Where are we going?" She asked, unable to contain her excitement.

"You'll see when we get there," he said with a big grin.

"So smug," she mumbled, but the smile didn't leave her lips.

They parked on a street before Reece hopped out and opened her door. She took his hand gently as he helped her out of the car. They started heading towards a white building. There were small lights in the bushes and strung around the black railing. She slipped her arm in Reece's as they walked up to the building.

"An art gallery? I thought that wasn't you," she said with a raised brow.

Reece laughed. "No, I don't own this one. I actually made an investment here for a friend, but she owns it. I just thought you'd like to see that not all of what I told you before was a lie. I really do have a passion for art."

When they stepped inside of the door, Reece reached inside

of his jacket before he handed a ticket to a man standing behind a podium. Janelle was too busy gazing around the room. The walls were stark white with paintings spaced every few inches. The lighting was soft and warm. Janelle could even make out the faint smell of what she thought was magnolia blossoms.

If the building was impressive, the people were even more so. Women in long dresses, men in tailored suits. They chatted easily with long stemmed champagne glasses in their hands. Servers walked around the room with silver trays of food.

"What do you think?" Reece whispered in her ear, making her jump.

"I think it's...different," she said, laughing nervously, "but it's very nice too."

"Here," he said, passing her a champagne glass, "let's look at some art."

Janelle nodded. Once again, she took his arm. They walked around slowly, Reece pointing out his favorite pieces. He seemed to like the paintings that captured lighter tones, happier moments, while Janelle found herself drawn to the moody, sensual paintings.

One contained a woman, blindfolded. Her arms stretched above her head. Janelle could almost see the woman's back arching up off of the blue, satin sheet beneath her. Her breasts pointed up to the sky, her mouth fell open in an unheard gasp. Janelle felt her thighs clench together a little tighter.

"You like that one, huh?" Reece whispered close to her ear.

Janelle nodded. "It's beautiful. I've always wanted to do something like that, but I've never been comfortable enough with anyone to try it."

Reece nodded. "We'll add it to the list."

She shook her head. "And who said I was comfortable enough with you?"

"You aren't?"

The look in his eyes was enough to make her want to quiver all over. He rested a hand on her lower back as he steered her on to the next picture. When they had almost reached the end of the gallery, Janelle was on her third glass of champagne, a woman walked up to them with a broad smile.

"Reece! I'm so happy you could make it," she said hugging him. When she pulled back, she smiled at Janelle, extending a delicate, but slightly paint stained, hand. "You must be Janelle. I'm a big fan of your show."

Janelle blushed. "Thank you."

"I'm Carrie," the woman said, gesturing behind her, "and these are my babies. Come on, I'll show you two the new pieces that I won't be putting out until next week."

Reece and Janelle followed behind her into the woman's studio. She was upbeat and friendly, with blonde hair that spilled over her shoulders, big blue eyes and a wide grin. The dress she wore was a dark blue and hugged her tiny waist snugly.

"These are wonderful," Reece was saying to Carrie as he gazed at the new paintings, "I need to buy a few from you again, soon."

"No problem. If you want, I can paint you anything, something new. I could even paint you," she said to a wide eyed Janelle. "What do you say? You have an amazing figure. I'd love to have you model for me sometime."

Janelle was flustered. "I-I don't know what to say," she said with a laugh.

The woman took her hands. "Say yes! I'm so happy that Reece has such a sweet woman on his arm now. It would really be a lot of fun to paint you."

Janelle nodded. "Okay," she said with a smile.

"Great!" Carrie clapped her hands together. "That's wonderful news. Reece can give you my number. Oh, Dyanara is looking for me, I have to go. We'll set something up," she called to Janelle as she walked over quickly to a black haired woman with a serious face.

"Well, she's cheerful," Janelle said.

Reece laughed. "She always has been. Let's say hello to a few people and then head out."

"Where are we going next?"

"If I didn't tell you for first time, I'm sure not going to tell you now," he said with a chuckle.

Janelle narrowed her eyes at him. "Keep it up. You're going to be sleeping on the couch," she mumbled.

"I doubt that," he said as he pressed a kiss into her cheek.

Janelle met so many people that she couldn't even remember their names by the time they left. There was VP this, CO that. All of it made her head swim a bit. Yes, she was good at what she did, but these people were from a different planet. Her stomach growled anxiously.

"Don't worry, we're getting food next," Reece said as he slipped behind the steering wheel.

"Good," Janelle said relieved.

When they stepped into the restaurant, Janelle could immediately see it was an expensive place. The menu's were printed in French and the customers wore formal clothing. Reece led her to his favorite table before the waiter showed up to take their order.

"What do you want to eat?" Reece asked as he casually glanced over the menu.

"I can't read a word of this," she whispered as she leaned forward. "What do you like?"

"Hmm, I think the question is what *don't* I like here. You like duck though, right?"

Janelle nodded. "I haven't had it in a long time."

"Duck it is," Reece said as he shut his menu.

When their food order was placed and more champagne filled their glasses, Janelle sighed. She had to admit, it was fun. More luxurious than she was used to, but fun. Reece gazed at her.

"Are you going to explain now?" She said as she took a sip from her glass.

"Of course," he said, sitting his glass on the table. "What do you want to know?"

"Well you obviously don't paint," she started.

"Well, I do. Just not for a living."

"What do you do?" She asked curiously.

"I'm actually an investor. I've always known how to juggle money and where to put my money to help it grow. Wall street has been kind to me."

"So, what made you want to be on the show? I mean, I get that you said you didn't want women to want you for your money, but there has to be other ways to meet them."

Reece chuckled. "Probably so. I admit, it wasn't entirely a well thought out plan. I'd just broken up with another girlfriend who proved she was only after my wallet and I was feeling desperate. When I saw the advertisements for your show searching for bachelors, I just jumped."

Janelle nodded. "I guess I can understand that. You just wanted people to see you for who you were."

"Exactly," he said with a grin.

"You didn't lie about anything else though, right?" Janelle asked anxiously.

Reece thought for a moment. "I don't stay at a hotel and of course, that was only a loaner car. I have a house not far from here, actually. Other than that, no. Everything I told you was true."

Janelle could see that he was telling the truth just from looking into his eyes. She smiled. For a moment, she'd been afraid that perhaps he'd lied to her about everything, perhaps she didn't know the real him. Having reassurance that he wasn't about to suddenly change calmed her mind a bit.

"So, do you think you can forgive me?" He asked, cutting into her thoughts. "I really do love you, Janelle. I don't want you thinking that I'd ever lie to you."

Janelle smiled at him. "I believe you. I forgive you, too."

Their food was placed in front of them. Duck with vegetables that had been cooked in wine sauce. The aroma was amazing. For a moment, the conversation was put aside to make way for them eating. Both of them sliced the duck before popping a piece in their mouths.

"Oh my God," Janelle mumbled, "this is just...Mmmmm."

"Right?"

"Do you eat like this all of the time?" She asked as she slid a bite of potato in her mouth.

"Sometimes."

"How on earth could you stomach the junk that I like to eat?" She asked.

Reece laughed. "I like that food too. Besides, it was more about being with you than whatever we were doing."

The more they finished their meal, the more relaxed Janelle became. It was still Reece. He wasn't any different, he just had more money. Janelle cleared her plate before they both shared dessert, a beautiful Crème Brulee that Janelle couldn't get enough of. By the time they were done, Janelle was full of warm food and bubbly champagne.

"I think you're just trying to get me drunk," Janelle said as Reece helped her into the car.

"I told you to take it easy! You were the one who kept saying 'it's fine, it's fine,'" he said laughing.

Janelle laid her head on the back of the seat. She was warm all over, the champagne had gotten to her head. She liked it. Now that the show was over, she really could cut loose with Reese in the way that she'd always wanted to.

"What do you think," Reece asked as he began to drive away

from the restaurant, "your place? Or do you want to see my house?"

"Your house, definitely."

"My house it is."

Janelle slipped her hand inside of his. He gripped it firmly before pulling her hand up to his mouth where he placed a light kiss. Janelle couldn't contain her smile even if she'd wanted to. She hummed softly along with the radio as they drove, but she couldn't stop stealing glances at Reece, who seemed to do the same thing.

When they pulled up to Reece's house, Janelle's mouth dropped in awe. It was huge! She couldn't stop staring at it until they were inside of the garage where Reece's other cars sat looking sleek and luxurious.

"Wow," she mumbled, "you really are loaded. And here I was proud of my little mustang."

"Hey, I love that mustang," he said as he helped her out of the car. "Come on. I'll give you a tour."

Each room was more immaculate than the last. Reece took

his time showing them to her, letting her explore them at her leisure. When they reached his bedroom, she ran a hand over his thick comforter.

"Wow, I can't believe this is where you sleep every night."

"When I'm not at your place at least. I mean, yeah it's big, but it's kind of lonely, you know?"

Janelle did know. As much as she enjoyed her loft, she did miss having somebody to share it with. Mulder was great company, but it couldn't quite compare to a good conversation and warm arms to pull you in at night. She turned to Reece.

"This was one of the best nights of my life," she said softly.

"I'm glad I could give you that," he said as he walked over to her slowly.

Reece leaned forward until his mouth captured hers in a deep kiss. His tongue darted into her mouth making her moan. Suddenly, she wanted him more than she ever had before. She wanted his hands caressing the curves of her body. His mouth kissing every inch of her skin until she couldn't take the teasing anymore. Janelle wanted to feel him inside of her thrusting, shifting, filling her up.

He must have had the same ideas as his hands drifted to her dress. His hands pushed it off of her shoulders, the sleek material sliding effortlessly against her skin as it fell her from arms. She felt the dress pool around her ankles. Reece took a step back, admired her body.

"Damn," he whispered, "you're beautiful."

Janelle grinned. Reece was back in a moment, capturing her mouth in hungry kisses that left her weak in the knees and light in the head. She kicked the dress away as her arms circled around his neck. She could already feel the gathering wetness between her thighs.

As they kissed, Reece reached a hand between her legs. His fingers brushed over the material of her panties. She shuddered as he moaned against her mouth. His eager fingertips pushed the panties aside before he ran a finger over her pussy. He moaned again when he felt how wet she was.

Janelle's body craved him. Her hands slid up his chest, pushed the suit jacket down his arms. When it had dropped to the floor, he reached up quickly to undo his tie, but he didn't let it fall. Instead, he draped it over her shoulders before his hands traveled down her back to undo her bra. It fell off to join the rest of their clothes.

Reece pulled back, took her hand. He led her over to the bed before he laid her down on it. Gently, he pulled the tie from her before he covered her eyes. Janelle's vision was taken over by darkness making her squirm with anticipation.

"What's this?" She whispered.

"It's what you wanted. Part of it, anyway."

Janelle could feel the bed move as he climbed up on it. He ran his hands over her feet with the heels still on them. Up his hands traveled. He passed over her thighs, over her belly, over her breasts. Then his touch disappeared. The excitement was almost too much for Janelle to bear.

Without warning, Reece's warm mouth circled her left nipple. Janelle gasped. His right hand traveled along her flesh until he was twisting and kneading her right nipple between his fingertips. She moaned, her back arching up towards the sensations. Without sight, everything was heightened. Janelle reached a hand down to brush over her panties, but Reece pushed it away.

"Not yet," he said in a stern tone that almost made her toes curl.

Reece went back to his treatment. Sometimes, his mouth would travel to her thighs. Other times, his teeth would lightly graze her breasts. She was turned into a ball of moaning, writhing hips and longing. Janelle found herself squeezing her knees together tightly, her fingers wanting so badly to reach between them and tease her aching clit.

When he pulled away, she reached out for him. He was out of her reach, leaving her to groan in frustration. She bit her lip, held her breath as she tried to hear what he was doing. Very faintly, she could hear the sound of his pants being unzipped. She could hear the material sliding against his skin, being tossed to the floor.

The next thing she felt was his hand on the back of her neck, lifting her up, pushing her to her knees. She moaned as he brought her head forward. Her tongue darted out, ran over the head of his dick before she slipped him inside of her mouth inch by inch. She heard him moan deeply, his hand resting on her hair.

Janelle moaned around his dick, the thick member pulsing in her mouth. She slipped him as deep into her throat as she could before she slid back up. Every pass of her tongue as she did made him shiver, she could feel it when she planted her hands on his strong thighs. She twisted her head, sucking harder until he couldn't take anymore.

Reece pushed her back on the bed. She heard the familiar crumbling of a condom wrapper and her thighs began to squeeze together even harder in anticipation. Reece pushed her legs open and she felt his dick pushing inside of her. She moaned, gripping the sheets as if she was holding on for dear life. He moved slowly, letting every inch sink in deeper and deeper.

When he was nestled inside of her body, he pulled the blindfold from her eyes. Reece gazed down at her right away making her feel self-conscious. She quickly covered her body out of instinct, but he pushed her arms away. As his eyes roamed over her skin, she could see the admiration he had for every inch of her.

Without warning, he lifted her legs, leaned in closer and

started thrusting inside of her. Janelle's pussy clenched around his dick until she was moaning without inhibition. He leaned closer, pressed his lips to hers. His mouth devoured hers as he thrust harder, deeper. Her hands wrapped around his back until her nails began to drag against his skin.

"Shit," she found herself mumbling over and over, her fingers playing against her nipples as she gazed up at him through half closed eyes.

Reece picked her legs up, rested them on his shoulders. As he slipped even deeper inside of her, Janelle moaned deeply, her eyes closing as he began to thrust into her once again. The feeling was almost overpowering, but Reece wouldn't let her get away even for a moment.

"Oh, shit," Janelle began to moan again and again as Reece drove into her.

She could feel the impending orgasm approaching. The muscles in her legs and stomach tightened. Janelle's mouth fell open, her eyes unfocused as she felt it rip through her body. Reece still didn't stop.

He really began to thrust into her. She cried out as his deep moaning filled the room making her toes curl. She gazed up at him as she felt another orgasm about to wash over her. He was biting his lip, eyes only half opened as he gazed down at her body sliding against the sheets as he fucked her. He groaned deeply, his dick twitching as he came.

"Wow," Janelle mumbled.

Chapter 6

"Are you serious?" Clark asked, a glass of white wine in his hand as he raised an eyebrow at her.

Janelle bit her lip before she nodded her head. "Why would I lie? I really think I love him too."

Clark grinned. "Awww, young love. I better be included in the wedding preparations bitch."

She laughed. "Of course. When there *are* wedding preparations...or if. We did just start dating."

He took a sip of his wine before rolling his eyes. "Oh please. That man is completely in love with you. It's only a matter of time. Trust me."

Janelle wasn't sure how she felt about that. After all, they'd only been dating officially for a week. She wasn't quite prepared to talk about or even think about marriage. Spending time with Reece was amazing, but marriage had never really been part of the agenda.

"Then you can have lots of fat babies," Clark was saying as he refilled his glass bringing Janelle out of her daydreaming.

"Babies? Oh no, definitely not! You know I don't want kids."

"He might," Clark said pointedly.

Janelle shrugged. "I'm sure we have more than enough time to cross that bridge when we get to it."

There was a knock on the door that broke their conversation. Janelle grinned. She pushed off of her bar stool before she walked over to the door, adjusting her clothes and hair quickly as she went. She could hear Clark chuckling behind her. Throwing him a threatening look, she opened the door.

"Hey, beautiful," Reece said with a grin. "These are for you."

He held out a bouquet of delicate, pink petunias. Janelle took them with a smile before she smelled them. The perfume from the flowers filled her nose. She sighed.

"They're beautiful," she said before she stepped to the side. "Come on in. Clark's already here."

"Hey, Clark," Reece called as he walked into the house.

Janelle let them two of them talk as she carried the flowers into the kitchen. She found a vase stored in one of her cabinets that she filled with water. Slipping the flowers into the vase, she carried it back out to the living room.

"So, we're all meeting at Reece's place tomorrow night?" Clark asked.

"Yep," Janelle said with a nod, "it'll be a nice little party. After all, we killed the estimated numbers for ratings. I think we could use a little fun time."

"I'm with you," Clark said with a grin. "Can I bring tequila?"

Janelle laughed. "Sure. I'm pretty positive Mya could appreciate that."

"I meant for me."

"Don't you have somewhere to be?" Janelle asked rolling her eyes.

"Ooh, yes actually," he said glancing at his phone. "I have a date. I'll see both of you tomorrow. Can't wait to see the house Reece."

"Out," Janelle pointed to the door.

Clark waved on his way out the door. Janelle shook her head. She knew he was teasing her about sleeping with Reece. The mere memory of that night made her shiver. Reece placed a hand on her shoulder.

"What are you thinking about?" He whispered into her ear.

"Your bed," she said with a grin. "And how comfortable it is."

"Oh? That's it?"

"Yes," she said swallowing thickly.

Reece wrapped his arm around her body. It slipped over her breasts, her belly, between her thighs. She bit her lip. He pushed up the hem of her purple dress before his hand slipped between her thighs.

"I thought we were going to talk party plans?" Janelle mumbled.

"Later. Much, much later."

Janelle giggled as she pushed him away. "Stop it! We have to focus, for once."

Reece chuckled. "Okay, okay. I'll behave, for now. As soon as the talking stops though, I'm carrying you upstairs and having my way with you."

She shook her head. "No objections there, troublemaker."

Janelle sat back down at the bar before she poured herself another glass of wine. Reece poured a glass for himself as she scanned over the notebook in front of her. There was a lot to be done, especially so short notice.

"Are you parents coming?" Reece asked.

Janelle nodded. "Yes," she said with a grin. "They're really proud of me. And they can't wait to meet you. Although..."

"Although what?" He asked, wrapping his arms around her.

"Don't you think it's a bit early to be meeting them. We've only been going out for a week."

"That's true, but we were getting to know each other longer than that, right?"

Janelle nodded before she smiled. "I suppose that's true."

"Yes, it is. So, relax. Don't go running away on me."

"You know me too well," Janelle said with a chuckle.

"Come on," he said pulling her up by the hand, "let's go out and get the rest of the stuff for the party. If it's not perfect, Clark's going to call us on it."

"He is a bitch," she said as he helped her into her jacket.

Reece chuckled. "I think he's hilarious."

"You would," she said as she locked the door.

Janelle hooked her arm around Reece's as they headed to his car. The ride was smooth as they drove along first to the floral shop to make sure that the flowers would be delivered on time. Then came a visit to the caterers to taste the food. She and Reece enjoyed that most.

"Try this," he said, slicing into a thick cut of steak that looked juicy. "I think you'll like it."

Janelle let him pop a piece into her mouth before she moaned.

It was amazing. Juicy, well seasoned, wonderful. She nodded enthusiastically, flashing thumbs up at Reece.

"I'll take that as it's amazing," he laughed.

"It was," she said with a smile. It quickly disappeared. "Oh, but that price. I mean, with the amount of people that are coming, that's going to be way over my budget."

"Yes, we'll take the filet mignon along with the side dishes we ordered. Oh and the cupcakes for dessert. We're also going to need twelve bottles of your best red wine," Reece said as he pulled out his credit card.

"What are you doing?" Janelle asked, pulling his arm back that held his card.

"I'm buying supplies for our party."

"I can't let you do that," she said with concern on her face.

"Why not? I want to," he handed his card to the cashier.

"Well, at least let me buy the other supplies."

Reece grinned. "Deal."

They set up a time for the caterer to arrive before they left the shop. Once they were back in the car, Janelle sighed. She didn't want Reece to think that she wanted his money or that she couldn't afford to pay for things herself. Still, she couldn't deny that he looked happy to do it. He still had a big grin on his face. Once they drove for a while, she looked around in confusion.

"I thought we were going to pick up the rest of the supplies for the party."

"We have to make a stop first," Reece said easily as he pulled up in front of a small ice cream shop. "Besides, I already bought all of the supplies yesterday."

Janelle narrowed her eyes. "You play dirty."
Reece kissed her cheek. She sighed. There was nothing that she could do about it now. He helped her out of the car before they walked inside. The rows of ice cream flavors were presented proudly. Reece was traditional and settled on vanilla in a cup.

"That's so boring," she teased.

"That's better than the impending disaster that you're about to order."

"What? Can I get chocolate, cookies and cream, cookie dough, peanut butter and cherry? In a bowl please."

"Disgusting," Reece said with a shake of his head.

"Shut up," she said elbowing him.

They took their ice cream to go, eating it as they walked down the street. It wasn't exactly hot enough for ice cream, but that rarely stopped them from enjoying their favorite treat. They ended up in the park sitting together on a bench. Orange, red and yellow leaves fell around them. Janelle leaned her head on Reece's shoulder.

"This is beautiful."

"You're beautiful," he said, placing a kiss on her forehead.

They ate their ice cream in silence as they stared out at the park around them. Janelle loved the fact that they could do that. Not every moment had to be filled up with empty conversation. They finished their ice cream before Reece helped her up. Janelle held on to his hand, not moving.

She wasn't quite sure why, but at that moment she knew that she had to tell him how she felt. It was a perfect moment, one that wouldn't come again to say what was on her mind. The woman took a deep breath.

"What's wrong?" Reece asked, concern written on his face.

"I have to tell you something."

"What is it?" He asked, curious now.

"I love you."

Reece smiled. "Well, it took you long enough to say it."

Janelle slapped his arm. "Asshole," she said walking away, her face hot.

He grabbed her arm before pulling her back to him. Grinning, he leaned down, pressed his lips to hers gently. Janelle leaned into him, her mouth moving against his effortlessly. She sighed.

"I love you too," Reece whispered when he pulled back.

Reece took her hand in his and refused to let it go for the rest of their walk. By the time the sun was threatening to set and the cold set in, they headed back to his car. Janelle had to admit, she felt relieved that she'd finally told him. She grinned.

*****

"Hey, where are the plates! I have to set the table," Janelle said in a panic.

Reece pulled them out before he began to set the table. He could tell she was nervous by the way she was running around. He was nervous as well. Her parents were coming to town, Daphne was coming over soon and through it all, there was the fact that he had more important things on his mind.

"Reece! Where are the napkins? I thought I put them in the dryer - here they are. Never mind."

He grinned to himself. She was cute when she was running around the way she was. Generally, she had everything under control, but he knew that she was nervous about meeting his parents too. Their worlds were coming together quickly. He just prayed that the transition would go smoothly.

Reece finished setting the table as she walked into the dining room, her heels tapping on the wooden floor. She set the napkins up on top of the plates neatly. Her fingers ran over the tablecloth, her lips moving without saying a word. Reece wrapped his arms around her.

"It's going to go perfectly," he whispered into her ear.

"I sure hope so because I'm pretty sure I'm going to pass out at any moment."

"You haven't eaten?"

"I'm too nervous," she said as she shook her head. "I will as soon as everyone gets here." There was a knock on the door. "I hope that's the servers," she mumbled to herself before she was gone once again.

Reese watched her answer the door. She was wearing a black cocktail dress that showed off her amazing legs. The black heels she wore almost made her as tall as he was. Her hair was in a bun, a few stray escapees curling down her neck. He wanted to reach out, brush the strands away.

"Oh good," she was saying, her voice filled with relief. "Just follow me into the kitchen."

The servers were dressed in all black as they walked into Reece's house. Janelle directed them back to the kitchen before she turned to Reece. She grinned at him.

"Everything's starting to go smoothly," she said with a smile.

"I told you it would. You just needed to breathe," he said with a laugh.

"I'm just nervous. What if our families hate each other? Then what."

"Then we do whatever the hell we want to do, because we're adults," he teased.

Reece pulled her into a deep kiss. He didn't think he'd ever grow tired of kissing her lips. When they pulled away, both of them went their separate ways to get ready for the party. Janelle went to go apply her makeup and slip on another pair of earrings, while Reece went to finish getting dress.

The man settled on a blue, button up shirt rolling up the sleeves. His hair had been freshly cut and as he looked into the mirror, he smiled. Reaching into his top drawer, he pulled out the small, blue box. For a moment, he clutched it tightly before slipping it into the pocket of his pants. Tonight was the night

*****

"Hey!" Janelle called out as Clark walked in. "How are you? How was your date?"

"It was amazing! I'll have to give you the details later, " Clark said with a wink.

Janelle shook her head. She could already tell it would be interesting, but probably inappropriate. As he said, Clark had brought along a bottle of tequila for after dinner shots. She popped it in the freezer before she headed back out to the party.

"Hey, baby," a voice called.

Janelle turned around. Her parents were strolling through the door easily. Excited, she ran up to them, throwing her arms around their necks. Her parents never seemed to age, despite the graying of their hair. They were both tall, lean people with black hair. Her mother was dressed stunningly in a nude cocktail dress that hugged her hips, while her dad was dressed in slacks and a button up with a navy jacket.

"I'm so glad you guys could make it," she said as she pulled back.

"Of course, we wouldn't miss it for the world," her mother said with a smile.

"We loved the show, by the way," her dad grinned. "Where's that Reece?"

"Oh, he's right over there talking to Mya. Reece, come meet my parents."

Reece strolled over with a smile on his face. He shook her dad's hand before he gave her mom a hug. Janelle could see her mom's eyes roaming over him, appraising him. She shook her head. That woman would never change, always the therapist, she insisted on analyzing people.

"Reece, my dad Terry and my mom, Jacklyn."

"It's nice to meet you both," Reece said with a grin. "My parents are actually coming up right now. Once they're settled in, we were going to start dinner. Could I get either of you a glass of wine?"

"Yes, please," Jacklyn smiled, obviously having approved of Reece.

"I'll take one as well," Terry chimed it.

"Sounds good, I'll be right back." He kissed Janelle's cheek before he walked off towards the kitchen.

"He's a sweetheart," her mom said right away.

"I knew you guys would love him."

They wandered off, chatting about Reece as they walked around the room. She introduced them to her co-worker's before Reece came back with wine and joined them. Together, they all talked and chatted until the bell rang. Reece jogged to the door, excited.

"Mom, dad!" Reece said hugging them.

Janelle smiled as she walked over to them with her parents in tow. Both of them had an almost regal look about them. Janelle noticed that his mom wore expensive jewelry, her chestnut brown hair piled on top of her head with not a gray hair in sight. His father was the same way, black hair, no gray, a small smile on his lips. Behind them, there was a young woman that had black hair with blonde highlights. Janelle recognized her right away as Reece's younger sister.

"You must be Janelle!" Reece's dad called as he walked up to her to give her a hug. She could see right away where he got his outgoing nature from.

Once introductions had been made and everyone had a glass of wine in their hands, they headed over to the dining room to start eating. The food that came out was amazing, each dish more delicate and elegant than the last. Again, Janelle wondered how Reece could eat anything else once he'd tasted food like that.

Janelle was surprised with how easily conversation came between everyone. Mostly, there was laughter. She gazed around the table, a smile on her lips. Reece gripped her hand beneath the table, giving it a tight squeeze. She looked back at him, happier than she'd been in a very long time.

As dinner drew to a close, everyone gave contented sighs. Everyone was so full that they sat around a bit longer, lounging in their seats, sipping on wine. Janelle gazed up as Reece stood. He tapped the side of his wine glass with a spoon. Everyone stopped talking, their eyes going to his smiling face.

"Thank you. I wanted to just say that it's been amazing meeting all of you. I had a great time on the show and you all did a wonderful job. Even the interns," he nodded with his head getting chuckles from them. "However, I do have a very important question to ask."

Janelle watched as he set down his glass and the spoon. He reached into his pocket before he dropped down onto one knee. She covered her mouth quickly. What was he doing? Her voice wouldn't work as he pulled out a blue box. He opened it, showing off a large, diamond ring on a silver band.

"Janelle, I haven't been honest," he said with a smile, "I talked to your parents a few days ago and asked them if I could marry you. We set it up as a surprise for the party. Look, I know it's fast and a bit impulsive, but I love you. I can't imagine being with anyone besides you. You're smart, funny, beautiful, stubborn, I love everything about you. So, Janelle, what do you say? Will you marry me?"

Janelle's mind was going in a million different directions. On the one hand, she knew she loved Reece. She had from the first week that she'd met him. He was everything that she had ever wanted in a partner. Considerate, kind, responsible, silly, sweet. The man was the total package. Still, there was a nervous fluttering in her belly. They hadn't known each other long enough. Rushing into a marriage might not be a smart thing.

"We haven't known each other that long," she mumbled.

"Do you love me?" He asked.

"You know I do," she said, a soft smile on her lips.

"And I love you. So marry me."

Janelle bit her lip. She didn't want to jump into it, but she had to admit that she cared about him. More than she'd ever cared about anyone before. Reece was the only man she could ever see herself with.

"Well?" Clark asked, looking excited. "Are you going to answer the man?"

Janelle laughed, the tension in the room breaking as she did. What was she thinking? Of course she was going to marry him. She couldn't think of a solid reason not to anyway. Slowly, she nodded.

"Yes, I'll marry you," she said with a broad smile.

Reece grinned as he slipped the ring onto her finger. It fit perfectly. She leaned down, kissing him. Through closed eyes, she heard the sounds of cameras taking their pictures. Her lips smiled against his as they kissed. When they pulled back, his eyes capturing hers easily, everyone clapped.

"We're really doing this?" She whispered.

"Oh yeah," he laughed.

They were instantly wrapped up in an array of kissed cheeks, shook hands and hugs. Neither of them could stop grinning. Clark wrapped Janelle up in a hug so tight that she slapped his arms away.

"I told you I'd be planning a wedding before long!"

"You already knew, didn't you?" She asked with a raised brow.

"I might have found the ring when I was snooping one day."

Janelle rolled her eyes. "And you couldn't tell me?"

"Of course not! I had to see the look on your face when he

proposed," he said laughing.

"You're not helping me plan a thing. We're no longer best friends," Janelle said shaking her head.

Clark tried to comfort her as she was showered in more congratulations, but she ignored him. Tomorrow, she would ask for his help. For the night, she was going to let him suffer.

Chapter 7

"I don't know which way is up anymore," Janelle groaned as she leafed through her wedding binder. "I think this is a bit much for me."

"Nonsense," Clark said as he moved his phone away from his ear. "You've got this! Hello, yes, I need to speak to you about these flower arrangements."

Janelle sighed. She was glad Clark was enjoying planning her wedding, because she was at her wits end. The fall had quickly turned into freezing winter. All the while, Reece was in New York taking care of business. He'd kissed her on the forehead over a month ago telling her that he'd be back soon.

She wasn't exactly mad at Reece, at least he was helping when he could. Still, it was going to be a large wedding and it felt as though the February 14th wedding date was getting closer and closer. They'd both chosen it, but Janelle had no idea how quickly it would be coming up.

"Did you pick a color for the bridesmaids dresses yet?" Clark asked.

"No, I still can't decide. Daphne really likes the red, but Mya likes the black better."

"What do *you* like better?" Clark asking, cocking his brow.

"Vodka," she mumbled. When he rolled his eyes, she sighed. "The red, I guess."

"She says red it is. Yep. Of course, we'll meet you guys there in two hours. Bye."

"Who was that?" Janelle asked.

"That was Daphne. She's going to round up all of the bridesmaids and we're going dress shopping. You still haven't even picked your dress out yet. I already called your mom, she's on her way here."

Janelle shook her head. "I don't know what I'd do without you."

"Not a thing. You'd be getting married in an alley wearing a pair of jogging pants."

Janelle laughed. "I'm not that bad!"

"That's what you say. Girl, you need to start making some

decisions. After all this is your wedding, you need to make sure it's something you'll enjoy. Otherwise, what's the point?"

She nodded. "I hear what you're saying."

"Good. Now, go get ready. I found the most amazing little dress boutique. After we're done there we'll get shoes and jewelry too."

"Wait," Janelle said after she slipped from the bar stool. "Where's the budget at now?"

"None of your business," Clark countered, "Reece told me not to tell you a single figure. It's your wedding, it's supposed to be expensive. Now, go get ready before I have to fight you."

"Okay, okay. I'm going," she mumbled as she walked up the stairs to her room.

Janelle rumbled through her closets for a while before she settled on a pair of slacks and a white blouse. She pulled her hair into a ponytail, dabbed on a bit of makeup and was ready to go. When she walked back downstairs, her mom was already waiting downstairs. Janelle smiled as she hugged her.

"I missed you," Jacklyn said.

"I missed you too. Sorry, I haven't really had time to talk. This wedding planning is driving me crazy. I should have pushed the date back farther."

"It wouldn't matter, trust me. I had a year to plan your father and I's wedding. It still drove me to the brink of going crazy. Besides, you have all of us here to support you."

Janelle smiled. "Yeah, that's true. And having Clark around is like a one man army."

"Damn straight!" Clark called from the next room.

They laughed as Janelle slipped on her boots. She threw on the heavy, winter coat that Reece had bought her before they stepped outside. Snow covered the ground. Janelle wrapped her coat around herself a little tighter before digging into her pockets to pull out the pair of matching black gloves trimmed with fur.

Clark drove them to the boutique in his car. It wasn't far away and for that Janelle was glad. She had to admit, she was excited about going shopping for her dress. Unlike other women, she'd never dreamed about a wedding, she'd never really thought about it in fact. She was too busy planning her career. Now, she had no idea what kind of dress she wanted, but she knew she would know it when she found it.

The boutique had a wide selection of dresses that were all highly priced. As soon as Janelle began to protest, Clark cut her off and reminded her that Reece was taking care of it all. She sighed. Looking at them all though, she had to admit she admired them. They were beautiful.

She took a seat in a cream arm chair and was immediately handed a glass of champagne. For that she was grateful. She took a long sip of the bubbly drink as the bridesmaids picked out their dresses. Janelle approved each one before it was her turn to pick out a dress. She drained her champagne glass before she began to search through the racks.

A few caught her eye, but none of them were what she was looking for. She went past dresses that seemed as if they would hug every curve. Finally, her eyes stopped on one. She smiled.

"This one is beautiful," she said holding it up for her mom to see.

"Try it on!"

Janelle stepped into the dressing room and she shed her clothes. She stepped into the dress, calling her mom in when she couldn't zip it. Jacklyn zipped it up easily, smiling at her reflection in the mirror.

"You look beautiful," she whispered, her eyes already tearing up.

Janelle had to admit she was in love. The top of the dress had thin straps that laid against her skin comfortably. The top was beaded beautifully while the bottom was poofy. It made the bottom of the dress huge. A red ribbon went around the middle, the long tails lying against the skirt. Janelle felt like a princess as she ran her hands over the material.

"This is the one," she said smiling. "It's perfect."

"Well, let us see already!" Clark was calling from outside.

Janelle laughed. She gathered up the skirt before she stepped out into the room. Everyone's mouths dropped when they saw her. She beamed.

"I'll take that as you guys like it."

"You look beautiful!" Mya said as she walked over to her. "I love it. Reece is going to love it too."

"You do look amazing," Daphne chimed in.

"Ah, the ballgown," the sales woman said with a smile as she walked over. "It's a good choice. You look stunning."

"I'll take it," Janelle said.

"Lovely. I'll ring it up for you."

"Oh, we should pay for our dresses too. And Clark's suit," Mya said setting down her glass.

The woman shook her head. "No need. Mr. James has already taken care of everything. Congratulations on your upcoming nuptials," the woman said with a smile before she turned back towards the register.

"Have I said how much I love Reece lately?" Mya said laughing.

Janelle went back into the dressing room. She almost didn't want to take the dress off, but she slipped out of it so that it could be wrapped up. Wiggling back into her clothes, she couldn't help but to grin. After she was dressed, she dug into her bag for her phone.

"Okay ladies," Clark was saying behind her. "We have two more stops. Shoes then jewelry."

Janelle stepped outside as she called Reece. She bit her lip as his phone rang. It wasn't long of course before he picked up, his deep voice sending shivers down her spine even through the phone.

"Hello, beautiful."

"Hi handsome," she said. "Thanks for buying the dresses."

"I told you, I'm taking care of everything."

She laughed. "You did. I found an amazing dress."

"I know I'll love you in it."

"I miss you," Janelle said softly, trying to fight past the lump that had formed in her throat.

"I miss you too. And the good news is that I finished up work early. I should be seeing you very, *very* soon."

Relief flooded Janelle. They told each other goodbye before she stepped back into the warmth of the shop. Everyone was already all bundled up, ready to head to the next shop.

By the end of the day, Janelle was exhausted. She'd safely stored her dress at Clark's house so there was no way Reece would know what she'd be wearing. Her mom was heading to a hotel for the night. Janelle could tell that she was tired too. When she stepped through the front door of her apartment, she flipped on the lights. Sighing, she headed to the kitchen, wondering what she was going to eat.

"Hey."

Janelle jumped. Sitting on the couch, was Reece. He had a big grin on his face. Janelle ran over to him as he stood, throwing her arms around his neck. Without a word, he kissed her deeply. From that simple gesture, she could tell that he'd missed her just as much as she'd missed him.

"What are you doing here so early?" Janelle asked.

"I told you that I was coming home early," he said with a laugh.

"You didn't say this early!"

"I couldn't stand not being around you," he said as his hands ran over her face, pulling her into another kiss.

Janelle quickly lost her thoughts as she leaned against him. His hands were already eagerly roaming over her body. She already knew they wouldn't even make it upstairs as they sank to the couch.

*****

"Okay, what's on the agenda," Reece asked the next morning.

"Caterers. Our favorite thing in the world."

"Mmm, food," Reece said looking happy and dazed.

Janelle laughed. She already knew what was going through his head. He was thinking about all of the foods they would try. The rich sauces, the juicy meats, the amazing delicacies. She had to admit, she was just as excited as he was.

"We have to do cake testings today too," she added.

"Oh baby," he said as he kissed her. "Now, you're just teasing me."

They spent the next few hours sampling food from various caterers until they settled on a menu. When that was done, Reece was all but eagerly dragging her to the bakery. As soon as they'd stepped inside, they were hit with the smell of sugar, fruit and chocolate. Janelle couldn't wait.

Both of them took a seat at one of the tables before a man brought out a tray for them. On it, there were various slices of cake; strawberry, double chocolate, coconut, red velvet. Janelle wasn't sure where to start first.
"These look amazing," she said to the man.

He beamed. "I make every one from scratch and as you can see, I decorate them exactly to specifications. Enjoy them. I'll be back in a while to check on both of you."

"Thank you," they replied in unison before they began to dig in.

"Mmmm," Reece said as he bit into a piece of cake with butter cream frosting. "This one for sure."

Janelle tasted it. "Ew, I don't like it."

"Strange as usual," he sighed.

Janelle simply smiled as she bit into a piece of double chocolate. "This one?"

Reece shook his head. "Definitely not."

They went through each slice that way until they found one that they could both agree on. The raspberry chocolate was a delicious combination. Reece loved the sweetness, while she fell in love with the tart. Satisfied, they both approached the register to discuss the design and decoration of the cake.

"You both have healthy appetites," the baker said laughing, "your kids will be good eaters."

"Of course," Reece said with a smile.

At the same time, Janelle scoffed. "Yeah right."

They both stopped and stared at each other. Janelle's eyes went wide. She'd never realized that Reece wanted kids. Reece must have been thinking the same thing as he talked first.

"You don't want kids?"

"Definitely not," she said frowning.

"You said that you liked kids."

"I do," she said. "When I can give them back to their parents. Why on earth would you want kids?"

"Well, that's probably because I *actually* like kids."

Janelle folded her arms over her chest. "What is *that* supposed to mean?"

"It just means you lied about liking kids."

She scoffed. "I didn't lie. You just assumed I'd want to churn out babies apparently."

Reece shook his head. "I can't even believe we're having this conversation."

"We're not," Janelle said curtly, "I don't want kids. End of discussion."

Heated, she left out of the shop, the small bell overhead chiming as she left. She headed to the car. The whole day had taken a sour turn she hadn't expected. All she wanted to do was go home. Reece was several minutes before he jogged outside and unlocked the doors. He drove them back to her place, neither of them saying a word.

*****

Janelle wondered how long they were going to keep it up. The wedding was getting closer and they hadn't spoken in three days. Janelle was too stubborn to call him though. After the bakery, they'd gotten into another fight at her place that had resulted in Reece leaving, slamming the door behind him.

"I can't believe both of you are being this stupid," Clark said as he sat at the bar, a frown on his face.

Janelle rolled her eyes. "You just want to keep planning."

"Yes, I do! I want you to have a wedding," he said agitated. "Dumb ass," she heard him mumble.

"I heard that. And it's not my fault. How was I supposed to know that he'd want kids?"

"You could have asked," he said pointedly. "Besides, what the hell do you have against kids anyway?"

Janelle sighed. "I don't really have anything against them, per se. It's more that I don't want to sacrifice my career to have babies."

"Who said that you did?"

Janelle shrugged. "I don't know. I just don't want to take the chance."

"Janelle," Clark said slowly, pinching the bridge of his nose. "Your future husband is *rich*. I'm pretty sure you can hire a good nanny."

"What if I'm not good at it?" Janelle asked quietly.

"What do you mean?"

"What if I'm not a good mom? I mean, my mom was perfect. There's no way that I can be like her."

"It's not a competition," Clark said, laying a hand on hers. "You would make a great mom. What you need to be doing right now, is calling your fiance and having this discussion with him."

Janelle sighed. "Fine. I'll call him."

"Good. I'm going to leave so you can call him over. See you in the morning?"

"Yeah," she said walking him to the door. "Good night."

"Night," he called.

Janelle took a deep breath before she called Reece. He picked up quickly. For a moment, she was at a lost for what to say to say before she cleared her throat.

"Can you come over? I think we need to talk."

"You're breaking off the engagement?" Reece asked, his tone flat.

"No! What's the matter with you? Do you want me to?"

"Hell no! When you said we need to talk I just thought you were going to say that."

Janelle shook her head as she rested her head on the bar. "Can you please just come over instead of giving me heart attacks?"

"I'll be there in fifteen minutes."

wwww.SaucyRomanceBooks.com/RomanceBooks

"You live twenty minutes away."

"See you in fifteen."

"Reece-"

Janelle sighed. That man was going to be the death of her. She couldn't stop the smile that crept onto her lips. Janelle was almost sure that after she'd talked to him, things would go back to normal. That was what she couldn't wait for. Not talking to him had been torture.

Reece showed up in exactly fifteen minutes. He still looked nervous as he took off his coat and boots, leaving them by the door. Janelle was sitting on the couch. She patted the seat beside her.

"I want to call a truce," she said pushing him a glass of white wine.

"A truce?" He asked raising an eyebrow and picking up the glass of wine.

"Yes. A compromise," Janelle said. She explained to Reece what she'd told Clark. When she was done, she could see that Reece was looking more relieved. "So, I wanted to propose a deal. We can talk kids after we're married for three years and my career is stable. Then and *only* then will I consider kids."

"Four?" Reece asked.

"Two."

"Three," he said quickly.

Janelle narrowed her eyes at him. "You're pushing it."

Reece laughed. As he did, Janelle smiled. She'd missed that sound more than anything, his deep laugh. He leaned over, placed a kiss on her lips.

"Deal," he whispered. "Now, can we please get back to planning our wedding?"

*****

February 14th came a lot sooner than either of them were prepared for. Thanks to Clark, everything was going off smoothly. For that, Janelle was grateful. She and Reece hadn't seen each other for the past week. Her mom insisted it would make the day more special if they had a little space. It still didn't stop them from constantly texting each other.

More than anything, she wished that Reece could be by her side as she packed her bags to head to the church. She was nervous. Whenever she felt like this, he was the one who could whisper into her ear and make her forget what she was so concerned about in the first place.

Clark snapped his fingers. "Janelle! Wake up girl. It's time to go."

"I'm coming!" She yelled down the stairs.

The last of her bags were packed. Downstairs, she could hear everyone in her party getting ready. Her mom came upstairs to help her into her dress. Her hair was already done as well as her makeup and she was afraid she'd mess it up.

"You're going to be fine," Jacklyn said as she zipped her up into the dress.

"How do you know? We haven't even known each other for that long. What if we're moving too fast?"

Jacklyn cradled her cheek in her hand. "You're a smart girl. It's up to you. Do you want to marry him or not?"

"I love him," Janelle said as she turned back to the mirror, she smiled softly. "I can't imagine life without him now."

"See? You answered it yourself."

Janelle hugged her mom. They made their way downstairs to the bustling living and dining rooms. Everyone stopped when their eyes landed on Janelle. She couldn't help but to feel embarrassed from all of the attention directed at her.

"You look amazing," Clark said, filling the silence. He walked over to her, hugging her tightly. "Now, get your gorgeous self into the limo. We're already running late."

It took a few more minutes to get everyone ready before they were ready to head out of the door. The snow was still thick on the ground. Janelle slipped into a pair of boots and lifted her dress high with the bridesmaids help. When they were all tucked inside, Janelle sighed.

"Nervous?" Daphne asked.

"Very," Janelle replied. "I'll be okay though. I'm happy."

Daphne patted her hand. As they drove to the church, Janelle began to smile. Pretty soon, she'd be Mrs. James and she could spend the rest of her life with her best friend. How many people got to say that? Butterflies were in her stomach as she stepped out of the limo at the church. The photographer took a few shots of them all before they were ready to go inside.

Their first stop was a room reserved for them to finished getting ready. Janelle traded the boots for her red shoes. Her mom helped her put on her veil. Her dad was waiting for her in the hallway, already looking teary eyed. The closer it was getting to seeing Reece, the more excited she became.

Finally, the music was starting up. She clutched her bouquet to her chest tightly as in pairs, the bridesmaids and groomsmen began their walk. She wrapped an arm around her dad's, tears threatening to spill.

"Ready?" Her dad asked in a choked voice.

Janelle nodded. "Let's do it."

Chapter 8

Janelle walked into the church doors. People on both sides stood, smiles on their faces. Janelle couldn't focus on them though. Her eyes were glued to Reece. The look on his face was enough to make her get butterflies all over again. The closer she got, the more she could tell he was trying desperately to hold back tears. He lost that battle, wiping at his eyes.

Her dad left a kiss on her cheek before he went to sit beside his wife. Both of them were crying too. Janelle chuckled as she took Reece's hands. She fanned her eyes, trying to keep them dry. She wasn't having very much success.

"You look beautiful," Reece said. "I love you."

"I love you too," Janelle said, brushing at her cheeks.

For as long as the preparations for the wedding had taken, it seemed to all be over in mere moments. They'd each written their own vows; short, sweet and to the point. Janelle was pretty sure they wouldn't have been able to make it through anything longer.

"You may kiss your bride!" The priest announced, a smile stretched across his face.

Reece pulled her into his arms. His lips met hers making a shudder run down her spine. Applause erupted behind them.

When they pulled back, Reece placed another kiss to her forehead making her blush. She hadn't been sure at first, but it felt right. Marrying Reece was the best thing that had ever happened to her and she was grateful to have him.

She and Reece waved as they walked to their limo. He helped tuck her fluffy skirts inside before the driver closed the door. Smiling, both of them waved to their family and friends before they fell into another kiss.

"Hello, Mrs. James," Reece mumbled against her mouth.

"Hello, Mr. James," she said with a grin.

Both of them began laughing. The reception hall wasn't far. Once again, Janelle was being helped out of the limo, her hands lifting her skirt above the snow. The reception hall was grand with crystal chandeliers and wood and marble floors. Everything was decorated in white, black and red. Janelle grinned.

"Clark did a good job."

"Yeah, he did," Reece said taking her hand. "Ready to go have some fun?"

"Oh yeah," she laughed.

Their night was spent in a whirlwind of food, wine and family. Janelle danced until her feet hurt. By the end of the night, she had a smile stuck on her lips. Sighing, she leaned her head on Reece's shoulder.

"Ready to call it a night?" He asked softly.

Janelle nodded. "Yeah. We've got an early flight."

Reece grinned. "That's right. We sure do. Let's say our good night's."

By the time they reached their hotel, both of them were exhausted. Reece helped her out of her dress before they climbed into bed. Smiling, Reece leaned down, placing a kiss on her lips.

"No regrets?" He asked.

"Not a single one. Check back in a couple of years," she teased.

"Oh really? That's how you feel?"

Janelle giggled as he climbed on top of her. He reached over, turning off the lights as he slipped her bra and panties off. She moaned against his mouth.

"I thought you were tired," he said as he ran a hand over her legs.

"You give me plenty of energy."

Reece smiled. He kissed her so deeply that her toes curled. Janelle wrapped her arms around his neck. She had definitely made the right choice.

*****

"The car's here!" Janelle called hanging up the phone.

"About time. We're going to be late," he mumbled as he picked up her bags.

"Are you going to tell me where we're going yet?"

Reece laughed, shaking his head. "Of course not. It's a surprise. Come on, let's get going."

Janelle picked up her two smaller bags before they headed to the elevator. Through all of the wedding planning, the one thing Reece had insisted he do alone was plan the honeymoon. Janelle's curiosity was getting the better of her, the excitement almost overwhelming.

"You won't even give me a little clue?" She asked once they were downstairs and the bags were being packed into the trunk.

"Not even a little one," he said as he helped her into the car.

Janelle pouted. "That's not fair."

Reece laughed as they drove off. "You're such a baby. You'll find out soon enough."

"Fine," she said, smiling. She pressed a kiss to his cheek. "I'm so excited!"

When they arrived at the airport they were given the best

treatment. There was no waiting for them, no lines. Janelle was used to the usual hustle and bustle of traveling, not this. As they sat in a private lounge eating their breakfast, Janelle kept glancing at Reece.

"What?" He asked after he'd bitten into a croissant.

"I'm just not used to this kind of stuff, I guess," she said as she cut into her eggs.

Reece frowned. "Do you not like it?"

Janelle shook her head firmly. "I love it. You're just amazing."

Reece grinned. "It's better when you have someone to share it with."

He took her hand when it was time to board the plane. Janelle had always been a little afraid of flying. The thought of being so high above the ground was unnerving. Reece gave her hand another squeeze as they walked outside.

"Where are we going?"

"My private jet."

'Private jet,' she mouthed silently. Reece never seemed to run out of surprises. They boarded the small plane. Janelle looked around in awe. The space was open, carpeted in blue and looked relaxing. When they took their seats, they fastened in.

The take off was a little rough on Janelle, but by the time they were in the air she had calmed down once more. She looked around them curiously. A flight attendant walked over with a tray before she made her a martini.

"It's a bit early for one, don't you think?" Janelle asked as she took a tentative sip. "Mmm, that's good."

"We're on our honeymoon," Reece clinked his glass against hers, the liquor in his an amber color. "We can do whatever we want. Besides, we have a long flight ahead of us."

Janelle shrugged and drank her martini. She'd given up on trying to get Reece to disclose their destination. That didn't stop her from wondering as she peeked out of the window to look down at the fluffy white clouds surrounding them.

They watched movies until Janelle couldn't keep her eyes open anymore. She rested her head on Reece before drifting off. Her dreams were warm and pleasant until she felt someone shaking her shoulder. She popped one weary eye open. Reece was leaning close to her, a smile on his face as he took her hand.

"We're here."

Janelle yawned, stretching grandly in her seat. "Where's here?"

"Let's see if you can guess. How about that?"

Reece took her hand as they stepped off of the plane. A car was waiting for them. After Reece had helped someone place their bags in the trunk, he slid behind the wheel. Janelle glanced around them, searching for some clue for where they were. As soon as they had left the airport, she figured it out very quickly.

"Paris! We're in Paris," she said excitedly.

"You're right," Reece said with a grin. "What do you think? Do you like it?"

"I love it!" Janelle cried as she leaned over in her seat to place a kiss on his cheek.

Reece sighed. "Good, I'm glad."

Janelle could see the look of relief on his face. She smiled. Sometimes he had an innocent side of himself that she loved to catch glimpses of. Janelle pressed her hand into his.

"It's beautiful," she said gazing at the city.

It was a beautiful place. Snow still stuck to everything giving it a romantic look. The leftovers of yesterday's valentines day still hung around in some places. Janelle mentally made notes of the museums and cathedrals that she wanted to visit as they drove through the lightly populated streets.

When they reached the hotel, they were given a set of key cards to a suite on the top floor. A bellboy helped move their bags as they checked out their suite. It overlooked a wide range of the city, lights sparkling as the sun was starting to set. The suite itself was impressive with a large master bedroom, kitchen, living room and dining room, two bathrooms and a powder room. The main bathroom even held a hot tub for them to use. Janelle turned to Reece as the bellboy started speaking in rapid french.

"Oui," Reece said quickly, tipping the man. "Merci."

"What did he say?"

"You'll see," Reece said with a grin.

"You're so secretive," she laughed as she wrapped her arms around his neck. "Thank you. It's an amazing surprise. What should we do first?"

"Let's go get something to drink, then come back up in an hour," Reece said checking his phone.

"Why an hour?" Janelle raised an eyebrow.

"Damn it, woman. You're asking too many questions. Let's go already," Reece teased.

Janelle laughed, looping her arm through his. They took the elevator to the floor below. When they stepped outside, the cold air made both of them pull their coats a little tighter around themselves. They picked up their speed before they stopped in a small cafe.

Reece ordered both of them coffee and pastries. The pastries arrived first and both she and Reece made short work of them before the coffee was brought out. Janelle took a sip uncertainly, then nodded.

"It's good. Strong, but good. I still think I'm more of a tea person," she said with a laugh.

"It takes a while to get used to. Let's go to the art gallery next door. It'll let us kill a little more time. Besides, there are some great pieces there I really want you to see."

They walked over to the art gallery hand in hand. Janelle took her time gazing at each one. Most of them were in the same style that she'd admired from back home. Reece didn't rush her as she went from photo to photo examining every aspect of it. When they were done, they headed back to the hotel.

While they were gone two massage tables had been set up in the living room. Two women welcomed them before handing them robes and letting them get changed into them. Janelle was excited. She couldn't remember the last time she'd had a massage, but it was long overdue.

"You're amazing," she sighed as one of the women began to run her hands over her skin.

"I thought you needed some relaxation after all of the planning. I felt like I wasn't around enough."

Janelle gazed at him. "You're amazing, you know that?"

Reece grinned. "I love you too."

By the time the women were done rubbing them down, the dining room smelled faintly of massage oils. Reece thanked the women before they disappeared through the door with a wave. When it was just the two of them, he wrapped his arms around her.

"Come here, I have another surprise."

"You're spoiling me," she said with a grin.

Janelle followed him to the bedroom. In their absence it had been filled with burning candles. Rose petals lay on the floor and bed. The smell of roses filled Janelle's nose making her sigh happily.

"Thank you, Reece. Really," she said with a soft smile.

"Words aren't nearly enough," he said in a familiar deep tone that made her belly clench with anticipation. "You'll have to show me," he added with a wink.

Janelle had no problem with that. She shed the thick robe

she'd been wearing, letting it fall to the floor easily. Reece's eyes roamed over her nude body hungrily. The lust in his eyes alone made her wet. Her hands went to the tie in his robe and undid it. She pushed the robe off of his shoulders, letting it join hers.

Reece leaned down, pressed his mouth against hers. His tongue slipped between her lips and ran over hers. She moaned into his mouth as his hands explored her warm, smooth skin.

She pushed him away, only for a moment as she directed him towards the bed. Reece pulled the blanket aside, a rain of flower petals falling to the floor as he did. The man climbed onto the bed with Janelle close behind him. She crawled between his thighs.

A moan escaped Reece's mouth as soon as her hand traveled the length of his dick. She grinned. Bending over, she ran her tongue over his warm, already hardened flesh. Janelle could feel the shudder that passed through him, the muscles in his legs tightening beneath her palms as she lifted her head up and down.

Janelle took her time. She sped up only for a moment before

she returned to the long, languid sucking. Her eyes roamed over his body until her gaze met his. Reece's mouth had fallen open partly, the sight of the pleasure on his face making her even wetter. She shifted a hand between her thighs, running it over her clit as she began to twist her head.

She was whipping him into a frenzy, that much was obvious. Janelle loved that she knew just how to touch him, just how to twirl her tongue to make him lose his mind. Reece's hand rested on her hair, his fingers pushing through her black locks as she began to increase her speed. She took a deep breath, swallowed his dick into her throat. The moan that slipped from Reece's mouth was enough to make her want to climb on top of him at that very moment.

Instead, when she came up for air, Reece sat up quickly. Before she could register what was happening, she was on her back. His hands ran over her breasts, his fingers pinching her nipples alternating between soft and rough. Janelle tried to run her fingers over her clit, but Reece pushed them away. It was his turn to tease her.

His mouth encircled first one breast then the other. The suction became stronger until her back arched away from the bed, her hands on the side of his head as she moaned. She could see the mischievousness in his eyes as he licked, pinched and sucked on her nipples.

As if that wasn't enough, he ran his tongue down her body slowly. When he stopped, it was between her thighs. Reece's warm, wet tongue ran over her slit, tasting her juices. He moaned before his tongue trailed back up to her clit. Janelle moaned when he dragged his tongue over it slowly, savoring the look on her face as he did. He followed it by flicking his tongue over her clit quickly, before sucking it.

Janelle was in a state of ecstasy, but it was frustrating too. She knew that he wanted to be inside of her, but he was putting it off for as long as possible to play with her. Moaning, her legs shuddered as an orgasm peeked, but he let it fade away. At that moment, Janelle had enough.

The woman moved quickly, pushing him into her place. Reece looked up at her surprised. Janelle climbed on top of him, gripping his dick before she slid it into her inch by inch. It felt like the first time they'd had sex, it'd been so long. His wide dick filled her up making her moan as it brushed against her g-spot.

Janelle slid up and down tentatively. The more her pussy relaxed around him, the faster she went. Every stroke made both of them moan. Janelle began to twist her hips in circles making Reece close his eyes, the pleasure on his face making her move faster. His hands reached up and gripped her breasts as she rode him.

Reece's hands slid down her body. His hands gripped her waist as he began to thrust up into her. Janelle cried out, her fingers running over her nipples. Reece gazed up at her, his eyes clouded with lust. She leaned forward. Reece took the opportunity to kiss her neck, nibble it lightly as he thrust up into her.

Janelle cried out as the orgasm washed over her. Her pussy clenched around his dick. The way it throbbed and twitched inside of her only made the orgasm feel better. She was panting as she rested her head on his shoulder, but Reece wasn't done.

The man laid her back, opened her legs. He ran a finger through her wetness before he pushed himself inside of her. Janelle cried out. She was sensitive all over, every sensation magnified from the orgasm that had shaken her to her core only moments before. His hands gripped her legs.

Reece pushed her ankles over his shoulders. Janelle felt every extra inch push inside of her, making her gasp. Reece started out slow, letting her adjust. It wasn't long before he really began to thrust inside of her.

The sound of him entering her again and again filled the room. Janelle couldn't stop moaning. Her hands gripped his arms tightly, her fingernails leaving little marks in his skin. Janelle loved the sound of him moaning right along with her.

Reece's breathing began to hitch. The throbbing of his dick inside of her made Janelle cum again. Reece wasn't far behind, filling her up as he moaned.

The man gazed down at her, a grin on his lips. "Worth the wait?" He teased.

Janelle laughed. "Definitely worth the wait."

Reece helped her to the bathroom when she was steady on her legs. He turned on the shower, the water steaming up the large bathroom. Janelle sighed beneath the warm spray. It felt amazing.

Reece stepped in after her. He took his time washing every inch of her skin with the loofah before she did the same for him. When both of them were freshly scrubbed, smelling good and satisfied, they stepped out of the shower.

"I'm starving," Janelle said as she wrapped a towel around herself. "Dinner?"

"Up to you. We can go out or I can cook."

"Let's go out later," she said quickly, "I don't want to leave this room for the next few hours."

"We've got all of the time in the world," Reece said as he lifted her chin. He placed a kiss on her lips. "Cooking it is. Want to help me?"

"You know it."

They both changed into comfortable clothes before they walked into the kitchen. Reece reached into the refrigerator and pulled out a bottle of champagne. Two champagne glasses were retrieved from the freezer before he filled them both.

"To us," Janelle said.

"To us," he repeated.

They clinked their glasses together as they grinned. Both of them took deep sips. Janelle sat on top of the counter as Reece began to pull out ingredients for dinner.

Janelle watched him with a smile on her lips. Even after everything that had happened, she couldn't believe that they had made it here. Still, she wouldn't take back a single moment of it, that she knew for sure.

When he'd taken everything out on the counter, Reece pulled out the cutting board. He started chopping mushrooms and peppers. She knew he'd wait to do the onions until she walked out of the room. Janelle hated the way they smelled raw. Happily, Janelle kicked her legs and sipped at her champagne.

"I don't think that's the right stuff," she said with a grin. "Are you sure you got everything?"

"Just do your job and judge the food," he replied.

Reece kissed her and she smiled.

The end.

If you enjoyed this ebook and want me to keep writing more, please leave a review of it on the store where you bought it. By doing so you'll allow me more time to write these books for you as they'll get more exposure. So thank you. :)

Get Free Romance eBooks!

Hi there. As a special thank you for buying this book, for a limited time I want to send you some great ebooks completely **free of charge** directly to your email! You can get it by going to this page:

www.saucyromancebooks.com/physical

You can see a the cover of these books on the next page:

These ebooks are so exclusive you can't even buy them. When you download them I'll also send you updates when new books like this are available.

Again, that link is:

www.saucyromancebooks.com/physical

Now, if you enjoyed the book you just read, please leave a positive review of it where you bought it (e.g. Amazon). It'll help get it out there a lot more and mean I can continue writing these books for you. So thank you. :)

More Books By Ashlie Iwu

If you enjoyed that, you'll love Money Over Everything by Rochelle Williams (sample and description of what it's about below - search 'Money Over Everything by Rochelle Williams' on Amazon to get it now).

Description:

Ashlie is a dance teacher and lover of the community. Jerome is a street hustler that values money over everything. Their worlds are about to collide, and this is their story. When Ashlie Sanders meets Jerome, a self identified hustler, her first instinct is to stay away. But as she gets to know him, she begins to see there's more to him than just his street smarts. The pair have a connection, a bond; and one that's unlike anything Ashlie has ever felt with another man. But while their draw is strong, Ashlie soon discovers it's very difficult to have a relationship with someone who is also married to the streets. Can she help Jerome become the good man she knows he can be? Or will she find the things she values most in life become casualties of Jerome's hustler ways?

Sample:

"Sharee, you need to stretch more," the voice carried through the small studio, over to where a young girl struggled to pull her body upright. Her teacher smiled, moving over to her, through the lines of teenage girls that were practicing with a worn ballet barre.

"Aw, Ms. Ashlie, I'm not all graceful like you,"

Ashlie Sanders was tall and willowy looking. With cocoa colored skin and bright hazel eyes. She did move gracefully, a testament to the years she'd spent devoting herself to dance. She wore blue leggings, with a gray, cowl-neck sweater, her bare feet hardly making a sound against the soft hardwood floors.

"Don't worry, Sharee, you'll be better than me if you keep practicing." Ashlie helped the girl move into the correct position, "See, that feels better, right?"

"Yes, Ms. Ashlie."

Ashlies' studio wasn't big, but it was all hers and that was just how she liked it. Once all the students had left for the day, she took to cleaning the big wall of glass mirrors. When she bought it six years ago,the studio had been a dump. If not for all the loving people that had made donations of money, or even their own hard work, Ashlie knew she wouldn't have ever gotten started.

Three times a week, Ashlie held free dance classes for the kids that otherwise couldn't afford the classes. On the other days, she taught dance to boys and girls that ranged in age from 5 to 18. Another instructor worked with her, helping Ashlie run her business smoothly: Keisha, her friend from college. She was a firecracker of a woman, who had a "no nonsense" policy when it came to dance and all manners of money making. Keisha's strict teachings, and Ashlie's love for the craft made them the perfect business partners.

"Girl, I swear if Carlos' dad looks at my ass one more time," Keisha said, walking into the studio with her hands on her hips. "I mean, I know it looks good, but damn." The other woman was a bit taller than Ashlie, with curvier hips, and skin as smooth and luscious as dark chocolate. The pair had been roommates all through college. Both women had a passion for dance that was borderline obsessive. Ashlie liked the fact that Keisha understood her need to give back to the community that had helped to raise her.

"You know you like him lookin' at it." Ashlie teased, as she sprayed down the mirrors with glass cleaner.

"He's okay," She said, moving to help, "But his crazy ex isn't. Comin' in here giving me the eye. Don't let the college degree fool you, bitch."

"You're crazy," Ashlie laughed. "Is Tina still having that kickback later?"

"Yeah, supposed to start at 8, but knowing her she won't be ready until 10:30." Keisha paused, "Wait, you're actually going to come to one of Tina's parties?" The disbelief on her face was comical.

"What's that supposed to mean?"

Keisha scoffed, "Ever since Mr. No-Job, you've been sitting at home watching Jeopardy."

"I have not!" Ashlie tried her best to sound hurt, but the reply came out as a laugh instead.

"Ashlie, yes you have; Jackie nearly forgot what you looked like," Keisha finished her side of the mirrors, then moved over to a large desk by the front door. She shuffled through a few papers, turning on the sleek laptop that sat on the desk.

"Ugh, I liked him," Ashlie protested, regretting the words the second they left her lips. Keisha was more than vocal when it came to her relationships. Though she kept a friendly perspective on things, Ashlie felt like she overstepped at times. Keisha was opinionated: coupled with her forthright attitude, it caused her to appear a bit mean at times. Ashlie tried not to let it bother her most of the time.

"Girl, he lied to you about his job!" Keisha yelled. "What kind of man does that?"

"He was just embarrassed…"

"Embarrassed, his ass should've been embarrassed." She shook her head, he curls flying loose from the bun at the top of her head. "I just want what's best for you, sweetie. Five years ago you wouldn't even look at a guy if he didn't have his shit worked out."

"Yeah, and where did that get me?"

"Don't settle, that's all I'm saying." She put a hand on her hip. "You're always trying to see the best in people. I'm just here to tell you that some people don't have a best."

Ashlie sighed as she reached up to undo her bun. "Some guys just need a little push, ya know. Need a fire lit under them."

"Yeah. That doesn't mean you have to be the one to light it. You treat boys like this shop: Fixer-uppers. You don't need someone that needs fixin'. You need a man that's going to take care of you."

"I can take care of myself," pressed Ashlie as she moved to

lock the doors. "I just think it's about time I settled down."

Keisha shook her head, throwing things into a duffle bag and picking up her keys. "Let's find you someone tonight then," she said firmly. "Wear something cute, bitch. We about to get chosen." With that, she was gone, leaving out the back door. Once she was alone, Ashlie went about making sure the studio was locked up tight. She'd picked a location that was closer to the suburbs than she'd originally planned. Ashlie had only gone to look at it because of near constant hounding from the real estate agent.

"You'll love it," He'd insisted.

In the end, the studio, with a little apartment above it, turned out to be exactly what she needed. Her family home back in the city was now near overrun with her sister's family. Brittanie, her husband, and their three kids lived in the small house willed to them by their father. While it had been home for a long time, Ashlie felt that Brittanie needed the space more than she did.

That apartment was her sanctuary. It was a small piece of heaven that she could retreat to whenever the world became too much. As much as Ashlie loved her studio: It was her's after all, the apartment was where she felt most at home.

Inside, the walls were painted either a gentle blue, or a relaxing green. The furniture soft looking, though minimal. Everything had a place, and Ashlie liked to keep her home neat and tidy. It was a mirror to how chaotic her life could be. She worked two jobs in order to finance her dreams; Sometimes it left her feeling out of control. At home, she could have things how she wanted, place things where she wanted, all while not having to worry about anyone else's input.

She went into her bedroom: The lonely space that had been devoid of any action for months now. Ashlie wasn't the kind of girl to mope, though. She was pretty and smart: Any guy would be lucky to have her. The issue came down to the guy being enough for Ashlie. She didn't want someone that just worked for her. Ashlie wanted a man that could compliment her. Whose desires, ambitions, and hopes mirrored and enhanced her own.

Sitting down on the bed, she kicked off her shoes, curling up on the soft duvet. There were a few hours until she had to get ready for the party, perhaps enough time to get a little nap in.

*****

Ashlie thought she was past the age where house parties were a regular occurrence. Yet, through some miracle, every weekend, Keisha was telling her about some party or another,

"It's not like how it was at school," she would insist. "Everyone's real mature, older, and all the guys are experienced."

Just like their school days, Ashlie walked into the house and felt immediately out of place. The dress she wore suddenly felt too short and the matching heels felt much too high. It wasn't that Ashlie didn't go out: She just made it a point to try to grow out of things. She was pushing thirty for goodness sakes!

"Hey, girl!" Keisha was on her in an instant, and Ashlie was instantly calmed by her presence. A cold bottle of beer was pressed into her hands: Ashlie took a deep swig, before turning to her friend. Keisha looked amazing in a purple sheath dress. It was accented by glittering beads and rhinestones on the collar, a line of which dipped down to show off her chest. The entire outfit was capped off with matching pair of heels.

Ashlie could see a few guys staring, even wished for a moment that she possessed her friends nonchalant attitude toward hook-ups.

"Any cute guys here?" She whispered.

"One or two," Keisha replied. "You-Know-Who asked about you earlier." And her eyes moved over to the corner of the room. Right past a group of good looking guys, when Ashlie saw who she was looking at, she nearly fell over. Sitting on a couch, talking to a small group of people Was a tall, dark-skinned man. He was dressed casually, but something about the way he was holding himself made him look much more dressed up. "Girl you know I like the bad boys. I would be all over that man if he had a job." Keisha fanned herself. "Why are all the good ones obsessed with the game?"

"Jerome is fine, though," Ashlie said. The man had lived near them once. One summer, Ashlie spent an alarming amount of time dodging questions from his friends about who she was dating. Jerome was exactly the type of man she was trying to avoid. He was dedicated to nothing but making money. And from what Ashlie heard, he didn't really care how he made it. He wasn't a thug, but he certainly wasn't a guy she wanted to get involved with.

Still, it had been a while since Ashlie had even talked to anyone. Maybe a quickie to get back into the game would help her relax and be accepting when the right guy came along.

Ashlie turned away from Jerome, moving her body so that it was up and just right. Since she was a dancer, she knew what made her look long and sinewy: Knew the right way to move to make any man not just look at her, but notice her.

Jerome had most certainly noticed. He walked over to where Ashlie stood, drink in hand, eyes fixated on her. He had the most startling brown eyes. They were a light brown, nearly hazel: Big, wide eyes, that at first, were much too innocent for his face. But they mellowed out, giving him a look that was more mischievous than innocent.

"Hey," Jerome said. "How've you been?"

There was a pause as Ashlie considered her answer. She wasn't sure what she wanted from him. Jerome wasn't her type. Ashlie told herself every time he flashed those sparkling white teeth of his. He wasn't stable, wasn't the kind of man she wanted. Yet, she wasn't sure if she just wanted to sleep with him. He'd always been a nice guy: A little rough around the edges, but he was polite and driven: Ashlie could see the potential in him from miles away.

"How are things going at that school of yours?" he asked, his voice smooth. "My lil' cousin Fay goes there on Thursdays."

"Fay is very talented." Ashlie replied, staring into the depths of her drink, "how've things been with you?"

Jerome shrugs. "Just trying to stay ahead of the game. Hard out here. But I'm doin' alright." He opens his mouth, then goes to stare at the contents of his cup. "How much your classes cost?"

"What?"

"How much. Fay likes 'em. I wanna try and get her in the real deal." His dark eyes wander to the far side of the room. "She's a good girl, I wanna do something nice for her, ya know. With her birthday comin' up…"

"I'll see what I can do," Ashlie said, sitting down on the couch beside him. "It's nice that you care for her: Not many guys would do that, even for their own child." It was nice: Refreshing to hear. Ashlie felt herself leaning forward, almost wanting to put a hand on his knee: Men that cared about kids were her weakness.

He shook his head. "Her dad and I are real close. Besides, I wanna give her the chance no one ever gave me. Let her do stuff the right way." There was a pause, "And it's an excuse to come see you."

She looked at him, lips turning up into a half smile. "What do you want to see me for?"

"Gorgeous girl like you? There's might be a couple of thing I'd want to see you for." He flashed those white teeth again, looked at her with those wide, almost innocent looking eyes.

Ashlie gulped down half her drink.

Ever since her father's death four years ago, Ashlie had been very erratic in her dating habits. While she swore up and down that she wanted a guy with a good job, she hardly ever got more than the grocery store manager.

A small part of her liked the 'projects' she called them. They were good guys with wayward dreams or bad guys she thought she could nurture into perfection. After the last disaster, Ashlie had made a promise to herself that the next guy she dated would be a man she and her father could be proud of: One she wouldn't have minded bringing home.

"Oh…" She said slowly, stopping the flirting, "that's nice."

"What, you seeing somebody?" Jerome sits up. "Your girl said you was single"

"I am but-"

"So there's no reason for you not to go out with me," he presses, reaching up to adjust the brim on his snapback.

Ashlie looked at him, her face fallen into a look of disbelief. "What if I don't want to go out with you?"

He looked at her, that same playful smile on his lips. For a moment, Ashlie didn't see the danger he could pose, and she forgot the whispers she'd heard about him. He's made her laugh, made her smile and feel comfortable and warm.

"Come on now. Every time we talk we hit it off." He held up his hands. "The only reason I never asked you out before was because you always seein' somebody. Thought you might wanna get to know me better."

"I know all I need to."

"Let me take you out," And Ashlie would never admit she found his persistence cute. "For real. Coffee, dinner, whatever, you name it. I'll even make a reservation somewhere." In his hand was his cell phone, he extended it to her.

She did like talking to him. They'd always chat at barbeques and cookouts, he wasn't like the rest of the neighborhood boys that just wanted a pretty girl on their arm. He exuded a strong confidence that ensnared Ashlie.

"You know what, fine," Ashlie took the phone. "I'll give you my number, and we can decide on a day and a time over another beer."

*****

Four afternoons a week, Ashlie helped out at a private school in the city. While the extra work made for some long, hellish days, the extra money allowed her to keep offering free classes at the studio. Plus, the kids were great.

It was an awesome community to work for: The school was very diverse, and catered to a huge population of gifted children, a lot of them coming from homes that usually wouldn't have been able to afford such a top tier school.

Ashlie worked with the younger kids, leading an after-school study program. In the mornings she worked at the studio, and then at three she would go to the school for a few hours.

It was at the end of one of those long days, she and Jerome had agreed to meet up. It wasn't ideal for her, but the students had a recital coming up, and the school was having conferences, so she wouldn't be free again for weeks.

"I cannot believe you are going out with him," Keisha said. The woman was perched on one of Ashlie's bar stools, brushing coats of polish over her nails. "I thought you said you were going after something different this time."

"He is different," said Ashlie, waltzing out of her room in a tight pair of jeans, and a blush colored blouse. "What about this?"

Her friend looked up, shaking her head, "Your girls are out to play." A small grin turned up the corner of her lips, "Unless you wanted him to get a little sneak peek." She turned serious again, "Really though, Jerome? All those fine ass men in that house, and you decide to go out with Jerome?" Keisha scoffs. "Why'd you even spend all last year ignoring him?"

"I was dating Daniel…" Ashlie reminds her as she wanders back into the bedroom to change.

"Now, I liked Daniel," she capped the bottle of nail polish and hopped off the bar stool. Keisha found Ashlie in her room, struggling into a pair of even tighter jeans. "I just don't want to see you hurt, Ash."

"How can one date hurt?" Ashlie looked up at her friend. "If it goes bad I delete his number. No harm done."

"I'm just saying, I don't want him turning into another one of your projects. Some men don't want to be fixed. He's grown as hell, walking around telling people he 'hustles' for a living."

"Yeah, that's not ideal," said Ashlie with a violent cringe. "I'm hoping he's just putting up a front."

"God, I hope so, or else he's gonna be asking you to put up bail money."

Keisha left twenty minutes before Jerome was supposed to show up. Only a few minutes after her car had pulled off into the street, Ashlie's phone buzzed.

Gonna B Late

Staring down at the text in awe, her mouth hanging open, and her face contorted in anger, Ashlie was sure at that moment she didn't look too attractive. A text. He was going to be late for their first date and he sent a text. It was all she could do not to throw the phone into the nearest wall.

'Calm down, Ash, she told herself, wishing that she'd made Keisha stay, 'he could have a flat.'

But the minutes ticked away, and after a half an hour, Ashlie thought about calling him. How desperate would that look? After an hour passed, she considered letting Keisha know what happened. The idea of the gloating vengeance her friend would dole out made her a bit queasy. Instead, Ashlie kicked off her shoes, peeled herself out of her jeans, and made herself a cup of lavender tea.

She would not cry: Her tears were much too good for a lowdown man like Jerome. Still, Ashlie couldn't help the feeling of sadness that overpowered the anger building in her gut.

She'd been excited, that was the truth. Now that the possibility of 'what-if' was gone, she couldn't help but feel down. Ashlie drained her cup of tea, letting the scent of it relax her into the cushions of her couch.

*****

The next day, as she was helping a curly haired girl do a proper plie, Keisha walked up to her, shaking her head.

"Someone's here for you," the woman said, a sly smile on her face.

"Who is it?" Ashlie stepped away from her student to look through to the waiting room. It was empty, except for a few parents waiting for their children.

"Girl, Jerome is outside," Keisha breathed, sounding more excited than Ashlie had ever heard. "It must have gone really well for him to be comin' to see you at work."

It had taken everything in her not to tell Keisha what

happened. When she'd come into the studio that morning, it was all she could do to avoid the questions.

Ashlie made him wait. Which was only fair considering he'd been the one to stand her up in the first place. Once the studio was empty, and Keisha had ducked away to go over some paperwork, Ashlie went outside, hoping that Jerome had gotten the message. The thirteen missed calls on her phone she'd woken up to hadn't been enough to appease her. Neither had the long voicemail she'd deleted without listening to. As far as Ashlie was concerned, anything that could have been with Jerome was now not a possibility.

Right in front of the studio doors, was Jerome. He was leaning against the door of a sleek, black sedan, wearing a crisp white button down, and a pair of jeans. Ashlie rolled her eyes when she saw him, not even wanting to go outside. A bouquet of red roses were tucked beneath his arm, and he held them up when he noticed her in the doorway.

He pushed away from the car, moving toward her. Ashlie wanted to turn away, but she held her ground, looking him dead in the eye.

"What do you want?" Her voice was low and cold.

"I just wanted to explain…" Jerome said, his voice sounding muffled through the glass. "Don't be like that, Ashlie."

"Don't be like what?" She wasn't going to yell; Not over some guy that didn't mean anything to her.

"Something came up. I had to take care of business." Jerome was standing right by the door now, his face nearly pressed into the glass. His eyes were wide, almost as if he was sincere. Ashlie sneered.

"You couldn't call or something." At last, she pushed the door open, snagging Jerome's expensive sneaker in the process: Ashlie smiled at that, before fixing the man with her best glare. "I waited for you. I got dressed for you. Only to get a fucking text. That's some bullshit, Jerome. I'm not starting out with anybody like that."

"I know, I'm sorry." He extended a hand to grab the door, most likely to keep her from slamming it in his face. "I fucked up and I know it wasn't a good way to start something…"

"You think I'm gonna forget and forgive just because

you come crawling back here?"

"No," He says, surprising Ashlie. "I think you're gonna forgive me because you know I mean it."

"I think you better leave, Jerome. I told you once before that you aren't the type of guy I want to be with. You fucked up your chance with me."

"Let me prove it." He pleaded. "Come on, just let me explain." He sighed, "I was trying to scrape up some money to get Fay into your classes. Something went bad and I had to deal with it." Jerome moved closer to the door, "Honest, just let me explain."

She shook her head. "Explain it to my ass, Jerome." With that, she was gone. Locking the door behind her and pulling the blinds closed.

*

Want to read more? Then search 'Money Over Everything Rochelle Williams' on Amazon to get it now.

Also available: The One For Her by J A Fielding (search 'The One For Her J A Fielding' on Amazon to get it now).

You can also see other related books by myself and other top romance authors at:

www.saucyromancebooks.com/romancebooks

CPSIA information can be obtained
at www.ICGtesting.com
Printed in the USA
LVOW04s1606310316

481609LV00022B/932/P